Beach Christmas

by Grace Greene

BEACH CHRISTMAS
A wintry novella
&
BEACH TOWEL
A sweet summer short story

Whatever the season ~ it's always a good
time for a love story and a trip to the
beach.

BEACH CHRISTMAS
A Novella

by
Grace Greene

Plus the sweet summer short story

BEACH TOWEL

Stories from Emerald Isle, NC

Kersey Creek Books
P.O. Box 6054
Ashland, VA 23005

Includes the novella, Beach Christmas, first released in the 2014 Sweet Christmas Kisses anthology; and the short story, Beach Towel, previously published in the 2011 Summer Shorts anthology.

Cover Design by Grace Greene

Print Release: October 2014
ISBN-13: 978-0-9884714-9-8
Digital Release: October 2014
ISBN-13: 978-0-9907740-0-6

This is a work of fiction. Characters, settings, names, and occurrences are a product of the author's imagination and bear no resemblance to any actual person, living or dead, places or settings and/or occurrences. Any incidences of resemblance are purely coincidental.

AUTHOR'S NOTE

The novella, BEACH CHRISTMAS, first appeared in the boxed set, SWEET CHRISTMAS KISSES in September 2014, and is being released here with the short story, BEACH TOWEL, which was first published in the anthology, SUMMER SHORTS, by Turquoise Morning Press in September 2011. BEACH TOWEL is being released here as a short story with some updates.

BEACH CHRISTMAS and BEACH TOWEL take place in Emerald Isle, NC.

It's always a good time for a love story and a trip to the beach.

ACKNOWLEDGEMENT

My love and sincere appreciation to my husband, family and friends for their encouragement and support.

Books by Grace Greene
Emerald Isle Novels
Love. Suspense. Inspiration.
BEACH RENTAL
(July 2011)
BEACH WINDS
(November 2013)
BEACH TOWEL (a short story)
(September 2014)
BEACH CHRISTMAS (a novella)
(October 2014)

Virginia Country Roads Novels
Love. Mystery. Suspense.
CUB CREEK
(April 2014)
A STRANGER IN WYNNEDOWER
(October 2012)
KINCAID'S HOPE
(January 2012)

BEACH CHRISTMAS

Jessie Dawson wants to bring her loved ones together again and plans the perfect Christmas for her family ~ without consulting them. Things don't go as planned, but a special delivery and a stranger from the past may cause her to rethink her Christmas wishes.

BEACH TOWEL

Instead of saying, "I do," Carrie runs away on her wedding day. She runs to the place where she always felt safe and loved, desperate to find a way to rebuild her life.

BEACH CHRISTMAS

Jessie Dawson blamed Thanksgiving for what happened at Christmas.

Her dining room table was large but to ensure plenty of room for the turkey and decorations, she'd added the leaf extension. The tablecloth was damask, the appliquéd placemats were an array of autumnal colors, and the turkey, golden brown and hot from the oven, had yet to deflate and wrinkle. Jess looked at her mother on the right, at her younger sister, Lila, on the left, then at the empty seats and the missing place settings.

That was her reality—those empty chairs around the table.

She picked up the carving knife and forced a smile. She'd never done the carving herself. It was a sad reminder of who was missing, but she'd get through this for her mother and sister. The knife sliced into the meat releasing steam and aroma.

Mama said, "This looks perfect, honey."

"Perfect for feeding an army," Lila complained as she waved at the bowls and platter. "Why did you make so much food for just the three of us?"

"We count, too." Jess took a deep breath and dialed back the emotion in her voice. "Thanksgiving isn't only happening at the lake."

Lake Anna. That's where Rob and Elaine and their children were today. With the in-laws.

Lila didn't respond. Her dark hair was drawn back and secured by a clip, but loose strands fell across her cheeks. Her hair was black like their father's. Jess had inherited her mother's flyaway brown curls.

She didn't know what her sister was stewing over, but Lila was seriously sulking. Jess hoped it was about Pete, the most recent boyfriend.

"How's Pete?" Jess asked as she passed the stuffing.

"Not here, that's how he is."

Maybe he had moved on. That would be a good thing.

"Here's some turkey." Jess forked a large slice onto her mother's plate. "Lila, can you please pass Mama the gravy?"

"No gravy for me, Jessie, honey."

"No gravy? But that's my specialty."

"My specialty seems to be getting wider, so I'm cutting back and making better choices."

"You sound like a commercial."

Mama waved her hand at Jess. "You take after your father. Slim as a reed. You can eat anything and never suffer for it, so I don't want to hear about it from you." She smiled to soften the words.

Jess pointed toward the serving bowls. "Cranberries?"

"Yes, please."

"Jellied?"

Before their mother could answer, Lila spoke. "She wants jellied, of course. Dad was the only one who liked it with the whole berries. Nobody else."

Lila glared at the offending bowl of cranberries and Jess was stunned into silence. Her sister was right. Only

Dad. Habit could be a powerful driver.

Mama turned to Lila. "What's wrong with you today?"

Lila's mouth dropped open. "How about a little sensitivity?"

"Well, I know it's not about cranberries since you don't like either style. Tell me what's wrong and then I'll be able to sympathize properly."

They heard buzzing. Lila looked down. Her phone was on the table next to her plate, vibrating. She picked it up and stared at the screen.

"Excuse me." She rose and left the room.

"Pete," Mama said.

"Did they argue or break up or something?"

She shrugged and shook her head. Jess placed a roll on her mother's plate and slid the butter dish closer.

"The table looks lovely, honey."

Lovely. She focused on cutting her food.

"What is it, Jessie?"

Jess set her knife and fork on the edge of the plate. "Nothing. Everything."

Mama touched her hand. "Honey, try not to let it bother you. The in-laws have to be considered, too."

"But this year of all years... Did they really have to spend Thanksgiving with Elaine's family?" Jess sighed. "I should check on Lila." She rose, sliding her chair back.

Her mother dropped her gaze. She smoothed her soft brown hair behind her ears. The light of the chandelier picked out the silvery highlights. Her voice was gentle and low, but her tone stopped Jess short.

"Last year," she said. "That was the most important year. We just didn't know it." She creased her napkin. "You never know which year will be the most important, not in advance. Only in retrospect. Only after you know what you've lost."

She nodded. "Now, go ahead and check on your sister."

Jess looked at her mother. She couldn't find the right words, so she turned away and went to find Lila.

She was on the side porch pacing the planks. She clutched her phone, pressing it against her cheek, not to her ear.

"What's up? You okay?"

"I'm fine." Lila stood taller. Her hand dropped to hang at her side, but she continued holding the phone.

Jess nodded toward the door. "Turkey dinner's getting cold."

Lila stared, her eyes slightly pink and puffy. "I'll be in shortly. Don't wait for me."

"We could." Jess put her hands on her hips. "We're already without Rob and Elaine and the kids, and Dad, of course. Should Mama and I go ahead without you, too?"

Lila blinked and bit her lip. She looked away, then slipped her phone into her jacket pocket. "Okay."

Jess followed Lila back to the dining room. None of them had been right since Dad died, including herself, but the empty chairs at the table seemed to blast the news like loudspeakers. The Dawson family wasn't merely changing, they were broken and drifting faster and faster away from each other. Decades of family memories and holiday traditions were fading fast, like old photos exposed to a cruel sun.

It took less than ten minutes to eat their fill. No one wanted to linger at the table. Jess rose silently and carried the dishes into the kitchen. Mama packed up the leftovers, sorting them into packages of three. Lila vanished again.

Only three. Three lone women.

What would Christmas look like?

Jess shuddered and dropped a pan. The metal clanged when it hit the tile floor.

Mama jumped. She spun around pressing a hand over her heart. "You okay, honey?"

"Fine. I'm just clumsy. Sorry I startled you." Jess picked up the pan and added it to the dishwasher.

From the kitchen doorway, Lila said, "I have to go."

They walked with her to the front door and waved goodbye as she drove away. The phone was back to her ear before she was out of sight.

Mama touched her daughter's face and asked, "Are you really okay, Jess?"

"You have to go, too?"

"I can stay awhile if you'd like company."

"Go."

"I can stay. Lucy said she was going to call today but if she misses me, she'll try again."

Jess retrieved her mother's purse and sweater. They saw each other often and there wasn't much to talk about except the same old news.

The wreath on the outside of the door rattled in the wind. It was turning chilly. What had happened to the warm day? Crazy time of year for weather, but that was the usual in Virginia.

Jess closed the door and faced the living room. Lots of furniture, perfect paint job, books in the bookcase, bric-a-brac arranged on gleaming wood table tops—her home was full of stuff, but empty. She straightened the

GRACE GREENE

chairs at the dining room table, tweaked a placemat into alignment, and then hit the switch to extinguish the chandelier.

Her laptop was on the drop-leaf side table next to the sofa. She propped her feet up on the footstool and settled the computer on her lap. She opened the lid and brought up her email.

In the sidebar where the ads ran, Jess saw the house.

It was an ad for beach house rentals. A special for the holidays.

The house in the ad reminded her of the coral-colored house her parents rented for Christmas when they were kids. Several years in a row, the Dawson gang had invaded Emerald Isle for Christmas week.

The beach in winter was quiet and private and personal. The kids played games and worked puzzles while Dad watched football and Mama read or crocheted. Instantly, the smell of freshly-popped popcorn and hot cocoa and the sharper tang of the evergreen tree in the corner swirled in the air around her. Back then, no one had argued. No one's heart was being broken. No one was left out.

Jess walked over to the bookcase. Framed family photographs lined the shelves. Some were from their beach Christmases all those years ago. She slid an old picture album from the bookcase.

Dad was always snapping photos in those days. There was daredevil Rob standing on the porch railing, and Mama holding baby Lila on her hip. In another shot, a group of kids, including her and Rob, chased the waves down by the water's edge. The local kids came and went, briefly fun and quickly forgotten. The core was Team Dawson and they didn't need anyone else.

She did an Internet search for Outer Banks rentals. There were several rental companies and many, many houses, but she remembered theirs well and found it easily.

It was the house. Still coral. In the picture it looked the same. A duplex, but rising tall, three stories, above the oceanfront at Emerald Isle. It was named Coral Cove. She'd forgotten that.

Twenty-five years. That was a sobering thought.

It was a big house. It would fit everyone, even with the addition of grandkids. She reached for the phone. Her hand hovered, then faltered and made its way back to the keyboard.

She couldn't assume the rest of the family would be okay with the plan. Besides, today was Thanksgiving. No one would be answering phones at the rental company.

Her family would be thrilled. It was a fabulous idea and would be a great surprise for everyone. The calendar on the webpage showed the house was available Christmas week. Jess nibbled her lower lip.

Available, but that could change at any moment.

The website offered an online form.

She'd grab the house now before someone else did. She'd tell the others later. It would be her treat so they could hardly complain. She'd send crafty note cards as invitations. It was going to be a blast.

With the smell of roasted turkey still lingering in the air, Jess filled out the form. She sensed Dad nearby. It was almost like she was a kid again with her loved ones around her.

It felt good.

****

Jess crafted the invitations with tiny shells and starfish cut-outs. She brushed glue across the front and sprinkled sand into it. She mailed the invitations and waited anxiously, eager for their answers.

Mama came over to the house and said, "Are you sure about this, honey?"

Rob telephoned and said, "Good idea. I'll take care of the tree."

Lila sent a text. "Ok."

Her boss wasn't happy at the short-notice request for a week off at Christmas, but Jess dug in her heels and insisted. Some things were worth risking everything for.

~ Five Days 'til Christmas ~

Jess drove across the long bridge from Swansboro and arrived in Emerald Isle ahead of the others. It wasn't a race. No one else was planning to arrive until the next day. After a stop at the rental office, she followed Emerald Drive to the house.

She had the road to herself so she drove leisurely and enjoyed the scenery. She'd never seen this road from a driver's viewpoint, plus time and weather had altered the sandy landscape and foliage, but even in winter it was generally familiar in a coastal sort of way. She was so busy looking that she almost missed her turn.

Coral—the color strong and warm in the bright daylight—how could she ever have forgotten it?

Seeing the house again, being here, felt almost like time travel, except the setting hadn't changed, only the traveler.

The house looked brightly tropical and huge. The sky was deep blue and the air was unseasonably warm. Delightful.

The steps rose steeply from the asphalt parking area at the back of the house, up along the side of the house until it reached the side door on the second level. She remembered those narrow wooden steps and how she'd clung to the railing as the wind, fresh off the ocean, whipped around the corner of the building.

But she'd remembered the stairs with a child's eye.

They weren't as steep as she recalled, but her used-to-be child's legs had aged twenty-five years. After the first trip up the stairs, she took a quick tour inside. After the second trip, she decided a break was due.

The interior had been redone. Different furniture, of course, but very similar. The style and colors were still beachy—turquoise and coral and sandy beige. The windows fronting the ocean were big and the view was unobstructed. White Carolina rockers graced the porch.

Jess went out to the porch. It had been a long time since she'd been to any beach.

She walked to the end of the crossover and greeted the ocean. Not quite warm enough for shorts, but close. Barbecue weather for Christmas, Dad would've said. Phantom voices, high and excited, rose all around, transporting her back. She soaked it in for a few minutes before getting back to business and resuming her trips up and down.

Mama would arrive tomorrow afternoon, Lila later that day, and Rob and his crew the next day.

For the rest of today it was her alone and she had lots to do to create a festive holiday spirit here for her family.

She unpacked the food first, including the entrée for Christmas dinner. It was a massive cut of tenderloin, solidly frozen now, but she put it into the fridge to begin the defrost countdown to the 25th.

Jess draped garland over the doors and curtain rods, and hung glittery stars from the base of the small chandelier over the dining table. She'd brought along some Christmas floral arrangements and her collection of Christmas candles, not to mention the usual red and green tapers with their holly and ivy holders.

Her phone was in her purse on the kitchen counter. With all the back and forth, and up and down, she didn't hear it ring. A voice mail waited for her to discover it, which she did after most of the decorating, and the evening, were done.

Rob's voice. "Jess, sorry. Janie has a fever. Let's give it a day and see what happens. It's probably nothing. I'll call you early tomorrow with an update."

Janie was in second grade. Prime territory for germs.

Still, kids got mysterious hit-and-run fevers all the time. She'd be fine by morning. No reason to assume her younger siblings, Rich and Suze, would come down with it, too. Rob and his family weren't even due here until day after tomorrow.

With that reassurance, Jess tidied up, her enthusiasm only slightly dampened. She saved the best bedroom for her mother, the same one her parents had used years ago. Jess took the next best. Rob and his crew could have the two bedrooms on the main level. It made sense with the kids. She left the topmost room for Lila who had younger legs. She could climb.

Jess arranged the photo album and a small stack of games and jigsaw puzzles on the coffee table. Before she turned in, she made the beds and hung towels in the bathrooms.

Nothing could spoil this Christmas. This was going to be great, an event to remember for a long time.

~ Four Days 'til Christmas ~

In the morning, Jess settled at the dining table with the beach Christmas photo album and flipped through the pages while she drank apple juice and ate a bagel, and waited for Rob to call.

By ten a.m. Jess was tip-tapping her fingernails on the table top. She checked her cell phone again to make sure the ringer was set to loud. Finally, she dialed Rob.

"Hey, Jess."

"Hey yourself. How's Janie?"

"She still has a fever and now Richie's down with it."

Silence. Jess let the air fill with nothing. She couldn't think of anything to say.

"Sis, I know you're disappointed. It's lousy when kids get sick for Christmas, but it happens."

"Christmas is several days away. They'll be well before then."

This time he held the silence, but for not as long. "Even if they're better in a couple of days it's a six hour drive to Emerald Isle. Six hours with kids who are just getting over something. We'd hardly be there before having to drive another six hours back."

She nearly bit through her lip. She tasted iron. No words were allowed out until she'd chosen the right ones.

"Jess?"

"Do your best, okay? It won't be the same without you all. Literally. That's not a platitude. Understand?"

"Sure. But no promises. Elaine won't like the idea of a trip with the kids having just been sick, that's even assuming they kick it quickly."

In that darker moment of disappointment, Jess couldn't help a thought that Elaine might not worry about a shorter trip, say, for instance, a drive that would take them to her parent's home on the lake for the holidays. It was a rotten little thought and it didn't matter how true it was, or wasn't. It was the kind of thought that could eat you alive, and solve nothing because 'not here' was still not here, no matter where the 'where' was.

Mama would be disappointed. And Lila. Christmas and the festivities lost a lot of their shine without excited kids, without stockings hanging low filled to their overflowing brims with goodies, without teasing about Santa, and without her favorite part—the reading of the Nativity Story. Dad read it aloud every year and his voice was so alive in her head it was as if his cheek was near her ear and she could feel the whisper of his breath.

Fresh from viewing the photo album, her resentment still sharp-edged despite knowing better, she slammed it closed, then patted the leather cover as if it could appreciate the apology.

"Sorry," she said.

She reminded herself there was value in a peaceful, reflective Christmas with loved ones, even if it was the same three people who'd shared Thanksgiving. If they had to, they could make it work.

Maybe they'd find a local midnight service. That would've been tricky with the little ones.

GRACE GREENE

It was always important to look on the bright side.

****

It was barely noon when Jess, in the midst of sorting through the food and checking the snacks, realized someone was on the porch. Through the front window, she saw a brown-haired woman seated in a rocker. Mama had arrived early.

She rushed to open the front door. "Hi. Why didn't you knock? I'm so glad to see you."

Jess bent over to hug her. Mama reached up to return the hug and they touched cheeks.

"It's such a beautiful day. I wanted to take it all in for a few minutes." She pointed to the wreath hanging on the post. "That sure is pretty."

Jess drew back and placed her hands on her mother's shoulders. She examined her face. She looked worried. Did she already know about Rob and his family?

"What's wrong?" Jess asked.

"It's so very beautiful and the weather is perfect, almost too perfect. It certainly brings back memories." She sat again and patted the rocker next to hers. "Won't you sit here with me?" She sighed and faced the ocean. She twisted her hands together. "Lucy called."

Jess sat, but leaned toward her mother and laid a hand on her arm. "Is Aunt Lucy okay?"

"Oh, sure. You won't believe what she said to me." She gave a half-laugh. "She said, Sister, I got a great deal on a last-minute cruise and you're already packed." She turned back to meet Jess's eyes. "And she's right, I guess."

"A cruise? Like after Christmas? For New Year's?"

"I'm afraid this will disappoint you, maybe hurt

22

you, and I wouldn't want to do that for the world, but this–" She waved her arms at the house. "It brings back many memories."

"That's the point."

She shook her head. "Too fresh, Jessie. It's still too new. I see your father here. It's like being back when you were children and we all had a future. Now…"

Jess hadn't thought of that. She was speechless. She'd been thinking of herself. Mama's grief was too fresh, too raw.

"I'm sorry. I didn't realize."

"The cruise goes to the Caribbean. It sails out of Charleston, so not much further to drive."

"Several hours. A couple, at least." Jess took a deep breath.

"Never mind, honey. You've worked hard to make all this happen. I'll tell Lucy we'll go another time. She can get someone else to go with her this trip."

Mama's eyes were teary. Hers were, too.

"It's okay." Jess put her arm around her mother's shoulders. "I should've known. I should've asked how you felt about having this holiday at the beach."

"Are you sure?"

Mama was going on a cruise. Over Christmas.

Jess took a deep breath. She nodded, then answered, "Definitely. Absolutely."

"I'd have to get back on the road right away." Mama checked her watch.

Jess gulped, then shook it off. "I'll walk you to your car. Do you have everything you need?"

"Yes. Lucy called yesterday. I didn't know what to do. I packed for either way. Going with Lucy or staying here, that is."

"Yesterday? Why didn't you tell me?"

"I wanted to say it to you, face to face. I'm so sorry, Jessie, honey. I don't want to ruin your holiday plans."

Jess stopped short. "No, you can't go."

"What?"

"I'm sorry, but even to go to the Caribbean, you need a passport now."

"No worries, honey. I got one a few months ago."

That stunned Jess. She let it go—the last squeaky hope her mother would stay. In that quiet moment, Mama kissed her cheek.

"Be sure to hug Rob and Elaine and the kids for me, okay?"

Jess nodded, not sure what to say.

"By the way, Lila is having some minor car trouble. We spoke this morning. She said it's nothing serious and she'll run by the repair shop and be on her way. She'll be a little delayed."

Jess watched her drive away. A passport? Her mother had never said a word about wanting to travel.

Her wave and smile lasted long enough for the car to reach the corner and turn out of sight, then her cheery demeanor sagged.

Now what?

She climbed the stairs and walked through the house. She couldn't settle. Packages of food were arrayed across the kitchen counters, but she couldn't dig up the will to re-engage with the Christmas prep. She wandered back to the porch and sat in the rocker again. A teary sniffle found its way out, but she shut it down. No self-pity was allowed.

The sun was strong, reflecting off the sand and water. There wasn't a wisp of breeze so the air was on the warm side of mild. Beautiful sunshine. Pristine sand. It was a pleasure to sit and rock on the porch. Or should've been. She bit her lip and worried it between her teeth. She'd stopped biting her nails years ago and her worry mannerisms had simply transferred.

"Ma'am?"

She heard a man's voice, but saw no one, only the pointy green top of a fir tree moving up into view as it ascended the steps.

"Hello?" she asked, as if the tree might explain itself.

The fir tree shimmied back and forth. The man carrying it climbed the last steps and maneuvered around the branches.

He smiled. His expression was open and charming. "Special delivery for the Dawson family." His hair was dark and his eyes were darker still. "Jessie? Jessie Dawson?"

"That's me." She crossed her arms. "Is that a tree?" Of course, it was. "What am I supposed to do with that?"

He stared, his expression suddenly blank except for a slight frown. "It's a Christmas tree. A spruce, I think. It itches."

As he spoke, in the back of her head she heard the echo of Rob's voice when he'd accepted the invitation to the beach. "I'll take care of the tree, sis," he'd said.

Great. Just Jess and the tree. Merry Christmas.

"Fine. Leave it out here."

Disbelief and puzzlement worked across his face like passing shadows and echoed in his voice. "Don't you want me to carry it in and set it up?"

"No."

He shifted the tree from one arm to the other. "You

25

mean, really leave it? Out here?" He looked around, then rested the tree, still upright, against the railing. "Be right back."

He took off down the stairs. Jess went to the rail and leaned over. "What are you doing?" she asked, but he was already gone.

She put her hands on either side of her head and pressed her fingers against her temples. How inconvenient. No, in honesty, it wasn't the inconvenience of an unwanted Christmas tree, but rather the tree was a conspicuous reminder of her failed plans.

The boards beneath her feet vibrated as she heard his boots hit the steps. He was carrying a red and green cardboard box.

"Here it is." He grinned, seeming irrationally pleased with himself and holding the box like a trophy.

"Here what is?"

"The tree stand. It comes with the tree."

"I don't need it. Never mind."

"Like I said, the tree comes with it." He knelt and right there on the porch he started securing the tree into the stand.

"I appreciate your work ethic, but I don't need a tree."

He stood. The tree was slightly atilt, but he seemed to have lost interest in the delivery. "What? Are you calling off Christmas or something?"

"I have no use for a tree."

They had a stare-down. During the eyeball to eyeball glare she noticed his hair could use a trim. His smile had been pleasant when he arrived—before she'd squelched the goodwill. She crossed her arms again, more tightly, and stood straighter because it didn't matter to her whether he was good-looking or not.

"Take it with you and give it to someone who can use it."

He continued to stare at her. She read it in his eyes when he reached a decision. "No, ma'am, Ms. Dawson. Nobody paid for a round trip for this tree. What you do with it is your business. Do you want me to carry it inside?"

"No."

"Have it your way." With a nod, he left the way he'd come.

Jess put her fists on her hips. Annoyed. Seriously. But he was gone now and there was no sense in being angry with him. He was a tree delivery man. Probably worked for the rental company. Just one more service rendered.

Sweet of Rob to arrange this. It would be much sweeter if he and his family actually made it here for Christmas.

She sat again in the rocker. The treads squeaked as she worked it back and forth. No matter how hard she stared at the ocean, she couldn't escape the sight of the tree. It filled the left side of her vision. The sharp smell of fresh evergreen assaulted her nose.

A couple strolled by on the beach. They raised their hands and waved. The tree had attracted their attention. They pointed, grinned, and waved again.

Jess smiled back, in chagrin, and returned their wave. In the beach world, was a Christmas tree on the porch, even if undecorated, the equivalent of a couch on the porch? Of course not. People decorated outdoors. Over the years she'd thrown a few lighted nets over a bush or two. Hadn't she hung a wreath on the post out here when she was decorating yesterday? Now the wreath had a tree for company.

Let the tree stay out here. She had no use for it. Not yet, anyway.

Later in the afternoon, she saw a box on the porch. Dented and scuffed, the cardboard box was stashed under the lower branches of the tree.

Jess lifted a flap. Sparkly garland was jumbled with ornaments. A crocheted candy cane was mixed in. She dropped the flap, stepped back and looked around. No one.

Unbelievable. This could only be the work of one person.

She tapped her foot. Really? Just as well he was long gone. She might have a word or two to say to him about this.

She'd brought her own box of ornaments but even those were likely to stay packed away. There was no point in hanging balls and bells and stringing garland through the branches if it was only for her.

****

After a half-hearted walk on the beach, and a return to the decorated, but lonely house, Jess dozed on the sofa. Knocking woke her. She sat up, disoriented, and then remembered where she was and why. The knocking came again and she rushed to the door.

Lila.

She wore dark leggings and a long, colorful top. A silk scarf was around her neck. Her coat was under her arm. She reached down to pick up the bags at her feet.

"Lila. You made it." Jess grabbed a small suitcase, then stepped aside.

"Of course. I told you I'd be here as soon as the car

was fixed."

"You told me? I don't think so. Mama told me."

"I left you a voicemail."

"Maybe I need new phone service or a new phone. I'm not getting my voicemails promptly these days. But you're here now. That's good."

She looked around. "Where's everybody?" She dropped her bags on the floor.

"I don't know where to start."

Lila stared. "Jump in anywhere."

"Mama went to visit Aunt Lucy."

"Lucy? In Charleston? Is she sick?"

"A cruise."

"What? No, wait." She held up her hand. "I need coffee. The last part of the drive nearly did me in."

"Sorry," Jess shrugged. "I don't have any. I'm not a coffee drinker. Mama was bringing her own, but..."

"She's with Lucy."

"I have cola."

"Bring it on."

When she returned with the bottle and a glass, Lila was staring fixedly toward the window.

Jess said, "It's beautiful, isn't it?" The afternoon was already fading to evening, especially early this time of year, but the sky was clear and the waves rushed to shore as if made to order.

"There's a tree on the porch." Lila walked up to the window as she unwound the scarf from her neck. "A fir tree. A Christmas tree," she amended. "In a stand." She turned examining the room. "Not in here. Did you need help getting it inside?"

"It's fine where it is. Our brother ordered it."

"Where is he? Out on the beach with the kids?" She

observed the room again. "I don't see any of the kids' litter. Don't tell me they went to Aunt Lucy's, too?"

"No, the kids are sick."

"When did you find out?"

Jess shrugged. "Yesterday. Last night actually." She sat the soda bottle on the kitchen counter and turned her back. "Would it have changed your plans if you'd known?"

A long silence.

Lila said, "So what is the plan, then?"

Jess turned back to face her. "Look, you don't have to stay. I know this isn't shaping up to be much of a Christmas."

"Which room is mine?"

"I was going to put you on the top floor, but take your pick. There's plenty of rooms to choose from."

As she headed up the stairs, Jess heard Lila mutter, "I'm thinking oceanfront."

Jess wandered back out to the porch and leaned against the railing.

Her mother was gone on a cruise. Rob was home with his wife and sick kids. Or maybe a better offer had come along for them, too.

Mentally, she stopped herself. There was no value to thinking that way. Pure poison. So, Rob and Elaine were home with sick kids. Maybe even sick themselves by now.

And Lila was here.

Lucky Jess.

~ Three Days 'til Christmas ~

In the morning, Jess reached for her robe before leaving the blankets. The bed was near the sliding doors and the cold night air had found its way in and around the panels. She donned her robe and slippers, shivered, and went to the balcony doors that overlooked the beach below. The chill emanating from the glass reminded her it was winter and only days until Christmas, but the sky was a high, pure blue and the morning clouds were such light, frivolous bits of fluff that it was hard to worry about the weather. As enjoyable as the mild weather was, did it really matter? Clearly, there wouldn't be any Dawson family events on the beach this Christmas.

The evening before that she'd spent with Lila was underwhelming. Jess felt the shadow of gloom still hovering. She'd tried to interest her sister in the photo album, but Lila flipped through the pages, frowning and remarking on how few photos she was in. Jess reminded her she was younger, only a toddler that last year at the beach. She pointed out the photos including Lila and told her what a cute baby she'd been.

She'd tried to interest her in a puzzle or a game. Even a book.

Lila had no interest in anything Jess had brought. Instead, she found a TV show about a group of annoying people. They were supposedly living in reality, but not in any kind of lifestyle that Jess recognized, or wanted to be part of. Lila settled in on the sofa. Jess saw the opportunity and said goodnight. It had been a relief to go up to bed.

This morning, a new day, would be better.

Downstairs, through the living room window on the ocean, she watched gusts pick up sand and throw it into the air like kids throwing dirt. The dunes grasses bent one way, then were whipped the other way. But the chill night air was already being pushed out by gulf air working its way north. Inside the house, it was too warm for the heat, yet too cool for the air conditioning, so Jess opened the front windows a few inches.

No sign of Lila yet. She'd sleep in this morning, no doubt.

The fir tree, semi-sheltered by the porch roof and the privacy panel, seemed okay for now, but if the weather was turning, she needed to make a decision.

But she already had, hadn't she? The tree was staying out here with the box which was still untouched under the lowest branches.

Jess stopped. She needed a mood adjustment. Only positive thoughts were allowed.

Something sparkly peeked from between the tree branches. She walked outside and moved around the tree to touch the lone ornament, a silver ball, hanging there alone. She asked aloud, "How'd you get here?"

A noise came from the far side of the privacy panel. Startled, Jess stood immobile. That half of the duplex was vacant.

A door closed and footsteps scraped on the porch boards. A man appeared around the end of the panel. He grinned. "Good morning, Ms. Dawson. How are you? Still want the tree outside?"

She stepped back from the tree. "I thought...I mean, what are you doing here? I thought this unit wasn't rented."

He had a quizzical look. "Does it matter?"

Jess shrugged and pretended to look away, "Of course not. I was surprised, that's all."

He leaned against the railing, but stayed on his side of the invisible line. "I'm working in there. Shouldn't disturb you." He left the railing and moved casually onto her side of the porch. He appeared to be making a point of viewing her through the foliage of the fir tree. "But let me know if I do."

Jess resented that he was making the tree part of the interaction, perhaps even trying to inject some levity.

"I'm sure you won't. Excuse me." She moved toward the door, but then stopped. This was silly. There was no excuse for such rude behavior.

She turned back toward him. "Sorry. Things aren't working out as I'd planned. I'm taking my frustration out on you."

He shrugged. "No problem."

"It's just that on top of the rest of the...plans not working out, you deliver a tree, a box of ornaments and you're working here next door. It's so...unexpected."

"It's the off-season."

He said it simply, unremarkably, as if it explained everything. And maybe it did. Odd jobs in the off-season. Maybe she was trying to make everything and everyone stay neatly in their assigned places. Where did Christmas tree delivery guys belong anyway? Why not next door?

He said, "I hope you don't mind me asking..."

Jess did mind, but trying to be nice, she nodded.

"It's a big house. You have people coming to spend the holidays down here with you, right?"

Jess tossed her head as if none of it mattered. "Sure. But there's been a few unforeseen issues. They're still coming, but some of them...may be late."

He seemed to seriously consider her answer, then said, "Glad it's working out. If you need anything, knock on the door. I'll be around." He finished with another grin, moved away from the railing, and disappeared behind the privacy panel.

She went into the house thinking about her too-friendly neighbor. Lila was standing just inside the door, holding her phone. Her dark hair was glossy and she'd braided some locks and arranged them artfully on the side.

"I like your hair that way."

"I was up on the balcony and overheard. He has a nice voice. Looks interesting."

"Are you?"

"Interested? Me? No. Maybe you should be."

"Thanks, but no thanks. He's a guy working on the unit next door, that's all."

"What's his name?"

Jess paused. "How would I know?"

"You could ask." Lila punctuated the words with a look.

Jess walked to the fridge. "Want some breakfast?"

"No, thanks. I'm going to find coffee." She looked around. "Where are my shoes? I thought I'd left them down here."

Jess reminded herself—only positive thoughts. She said. "Take the house key, just in case, and don't stay away too long. Rob and his family could arrive anytime."

Lila frowned. "Didn't you say Janie was sick?"

Jess took the butter and eggs from the fridge. "Kids bounce back quickly from these bugs. They might decide to surprise us. It's exactly the kind of thing Rob would do. They could've started driving first thing this morning."

"Jess."

"Please, you'd be as happy as me to see them drive up."

Lila was silent.

Jess asked, "Would you have come? If you knew the others..."

"You asked that before."

"You didn't answer."

"Fine. Would I have bailed on you if I'd known the others weren't coming? Left you sitting alone in this rental house for Christmas even though you deserve it because you arranged this on your own without asking anyone first?"

Ouch. "Okay. So that's true, but you know why."

"Sure, I know. It was a sweet, sentimental thing to do, but not considerate. It was controlling."

Lila pronounced the statement as if everyone agreed those were the facts. Controlling. They must've had a discussion among themselves, without including her, about her doing this for Christmas.

"Everyone was okay with it when I invited them."

"No one wanted to hurt you. We know how you felt about Dad. About him being gone and all."

"How I felt?" Her voice had risen nearly an octave. She pulled it back down to a more civil level. "We all felt his loss. It was hard on all of us."

Lila went silent again. Jess looked at her from the corner of her eye and saw Lila's attention had moved on. Lila was focused on her phone, her fingers moving at a fast rate over the keys.

"How's Pete?" Jess's tone was cold. She regretted the words immediately and wished she could grab them back.

Lila's eyes grew wide. "Are you trying to be hurtful? It's not like you're happy that we're seeing each other."

The question sounded rhetorical. Jess didn't think she expected an answer.

Lila didn't. She hit a key on her phone and then it was at her ear. She was already speaking as she climbed the stairs. Jess felt dismissed. Or maybe punished.

At the moment she'd spoken maybe she had wanted to hurt her sister—a swift hit back because Lila had hurt her and then started texting like it was nothing. It hurt that Lila, Rob and Mom had apparently discussed, in negative, critical terms, her arranging this Christmas trip to the beach. And disrespectful to their father because, in part, this trip was in his memory. It seemed that she, Jess, was the only who cared.

At the very least, she was the only one who cared about the trip. For the rest of it, Jess reminded herself that it wasn't Rob's fault that his kids were sick, and she couldn't blame her mother because her heart was still tender.

Jess moved forward with cooking breakfast. She couldn't remedy the coffee situation for her sister, but the smell of scrambled eggs would surely lure Lila back downstairs.

Someone knocked on the side door. Jess, excited,

moved the frying pan to a cold burner. As she rushed to answer the door she called up the stairs, "Lila, come down!" Her heart soared. She yanked the locks open and swung the door wide.

Pete.

Not Rob and the kids.

Pete. He stood there with a smirk on his face and holding a large cardboard cup with a lid, with steam escaping and smelling of coffee. The aroma hit her and she slammed the door shut.

"Jess."

Lila stared from the base of the stairs. Everything she felt flooded her face.

Jess's pulse rang in her ears and simmered at a low boil in her chest. "What's he doing here?"

"I don't know. I was talking to him on the phone. I guess he wanted to surprise me."

More knocking on the door.

"You have to let him in."

It wasn't manners or courtesy that moved Jess. It was the raw emotion on her sister's face. Jess groaned and opened the door. "Pete?"

"Hi, Jess. Are you going to shut it in my face again? Or, hey, here's a new concept—how about inviting me in?"

His sarcasm made her feel better. It erased her guilt over being rude. Pete deserved that and more.

"Don't tempt me." She stepped back and ushered him in.

Lila said, "I told you not to come."

"I missed you." Pete held out the cup. "Here you go. Can you believe how warm it is out there? Seems almost wrong. It's winter, after all."

"Pete." Lila stared at the cup.

"You said you needed coffee."

"But–"

"What? Did I do something wrong?" He seemed to be asking Lila, but was looking at Jess.

Lila said, "I told him not to come. I said we'd talk when I got home."

Pete moved further into the room, heading toward a chair. Lila took a step in his direction.

"Hold it, Pete. Not here. You two take this somewhere else. Or better yet, hash it out later, much later, after Christmas. After New Year's. Maybe after the fourth of July. But not here."

Pete turned his back on her to face Lila. Intended or not, he deliberately ignited Jess's personal bomb.

"Get out."

Lila hemmed, "Jess…"

"Out." She pointed toward the door. "I don't want the drama here. If you invited him, Lila, then take him elsewhere. If you didn't invite him, he can just go. Now."

Pete spun around to face her. "What did I ever do to you? When did you decide it was your job to run Lila's life? Not only Lila's, but everyone's."

"I have no interest in your life, running it or otherwise. Life isn't exciting enough for you. You invite drama in. You do that just by showing up here. For this house, for this week, I get to say what I want."

Pete's face flushed. "You always say whatever you want."

"No, I don't, and that isn't what I meant. I'm saying I make the rules here."

Lila's voice, soft and almost unheard, sliced

between them. "You always make the rules."

Jess stared at her. Wasn't she fighting for her sister? She was on Lila's side. Jess wanted to tell her... What? That she meant well?

"Not fair, Lila."

"I'll get my sweater." She looked at Pete. "Wait for me in the car."

"Whatever you want." Pete smiled and left. His feet pounded down the steps.

At least, Lila had found her shoes. Jess refused to ask how long she'd be gone. She clamped her jaws together and watched Lila leave with her sweater and her purse. She watched the door close behind her.

Even though her world was breaking into brittle pieces, Jess had to restrain herself from calling after her, "Take a coat. It could turn cold." Instead, she pressed her hands flat against the door as if to ensure it stayed closed.

She touched her forehead to the door and breathed deeply.

What do you do when you go away for the holidays, arrange a special celebration for your loved ones, and no one shows up? What do you do when you look around and confirm you are, indeed, alone?

The semi-tattered games they'd played twenty-five years ago, the worn corners of the game boxes taped to hold them together, were stacked on the coffee table. The draped garland, the candles on the window sills and tabletops, were still in place, but no longer festive.

Jess scraped the cold eggs onto a plate and took a fork from the drawer.

She could've saved herself the planning, the packing, the long drive, the toting of stuff up those steep, skinny stairs…which, she realized, she'd have to do all over again, but in reverse this time, with no holiday party, no pay-off, for the effort she'd put into the project. Instead of bringing her family back together, this disaster only emphasized the tragic truth.

Never mind the money spent and the probable damage done to her employment by insisting she had to take Christmas week off.

She toyed with the idea of calling Rob and decided against it. Why should she volunteer to receive more bad news?

Jess moved the eggs around with her fork. Unappealing. Her appetite had vanished.

All of this effort would have been worth it for a holiday with her family. If she'd wanted to be alone for Christmas, she could've stayed home.

Tears worked out of the corners of her eyes. She strode across the room and out the door to the porch. The salt air would dry up her tears and the ocean breeze would blow the frustration and anger from her brain.

Jess walked along the crossover. High-level clouds rolled in keeping pace with her edginess. The light wind blowing onshore was chilly but not cold. She walked to the end of the crossover and stood at the railing for a minute before kicking off her shoes and going down to the sand.

The dry sand was surprisingly, pleasantly warm beneath her feet. She dug in her toes as the grains shifted beneath her feet. The air was too warm for a December morning. The humidity was higher, perhaps growing as the atmosphere bunched up, caught between the tropical air moving north and the cold air plunging south. This bubble of unseasonable warmth was going to blow up sooner or later.

As was she.

No one was in sight up the beach. The opposite direction was also empty. The ocean was churning and white caps rode the waves on the incoming tide as they bashed ashore. The first cold, wet fingers of salt water rushed up the sand and touched her toes. Jess stretched her arms wide and, into the fury of the ocean, knowing the human sound would be swallowed up by the greater roar, she screamed her frustration.

When it was done and the last note sounded on the last expelled breath, she didn't feel any calmer, but thought she might have gained a sore throat.

The next lacy fringe of water snuck up. It rolled over her feet. Cold. Very. She jumped back a few steps.

Jess heard the boom of the wind before she saw it. It rolled up the strand kicking up sheets of sand as it came. Sharp specks began stinging her cheek. She flew up the stairs, scrambled to snag her shoes as she dashed past, not stopping until she reached the door. The branches of the fir tree shimmied in a gust. That lone ornament swung on a branch. Without hesitation, Jess opened the door and put it between her and the weather.

The tree rocked and the ball fell off and rolled across the boards. It was a good thing she didn't want this tree.

But was that true? Would it still be true tomorrow? Rob and Elaine and the kids might yet come and Rob had gone to the trouble of ordering the tree and having it delivered. She didn't want to disappoint him.

Another blast hit the tree and it danced.

Jess opened the door.

It was a big tree. In past years she'd moved her fully

decorated tree to tweak the position. She could do this. It wasn't a matter of strength, but of leverage.

She wrapped her hands around the trunk and rocked the tree toward her. Water spilled from the base and wet her feet as the tree passed the tipping point. She almost lost it, nearly went over backward with it, but despite the sandy, gritty wind, she focused. Gently rocking it back and forth, she maneuvered the tree through the doorway sacrificing the 'fir' on some of the outer limbs, to get it inside. Before slamming the door, she grabbed the cardboard box. She left it and the tree in the middle of the floor. She scratched her arms. They itched.

The tree was going right back outside as soon as the weather permitted, unless Rob arrived first.

****

The big wind brought rain with it, but only briefly. As soon as the shower stopped, someone knocked on the front door.

Her neighbor. She saw him through the large glass panel in the door.

She twisted the knob and opened it a few inches. "Hello?"

He looked beyond her at the tree standing in the middle of the room, then his gaze returned to her face.

"Sorry to interrupt. Just wanted to check on you. Everything okay?"

"It is, and no need to check on me."

His face pinked up and he looked down. "That's what I told myself, but I decided to risk embarrassment for me and annoyance from you. You screamed. Right before the rain started?"

"Screamed?" It was her turn to blush. Her cheeks felt warm.

"Well, yeah. When the wind blows off the ocean and toward the houses it carries the sound right along with it. But it was the slamming door that got my attention first. Well, after the shouting, that is. And followed by that scream, even though you looked okay when you ran back from the beach, I started to worry. If you're okay, and you do look good, I mean you seem fine, I'll go back next door."

"I am fine. Are you watching me?" A stalker. She had a stalker and maybe a peeping tom. "I don't know how or why you're so informed about what's going on over here, but it's creepy that you keep showing up and seem to know—"

"The windows were open. I was on the porch, my side. The voices were pretty loud."

Jess put a hand over her eyes. Was nothing private? She looked at him. She didn't know what to say.

"Every family has problems," he said.

Jess stared.

"All families have issues," he repeated.

"True." She felt off-balance.

"Anyway, I'm glad it worked out. It's good you took the tree inside because the weather's going to be unpredictable the next few days. There's another front working its way through."

"You deliver Christmas trees and weather forecasts, too?"

"Multi-talented." He nodded toward the tree. "Need any help getting it situated?"

"As soon as the rain passes, it's going back outside."

For the first time, real anger seemed to edge into his easy demeanor. His eyes narrowed in a squint and his frown pushed the good-natured concern right off of his face. He stepped back.

"You're hauling that tree in and out? Why? For what?"

"What's it to you anyway? It isn't any of your business."

"Apparently not and you've made that very clear. If I'd known it was going to cause you so much hassle, I wouldn't have brought it."

Jess corrected him. "You wouldn't have brought it if Rob hadn't ordered it."

He spoke softly, "Rob didn't order it."

She frowned. "But you said..."

"I said it was special delivery."

"Who then? If not Rob? Rob told me he was taking care of the tree."

"Maybe he intended to take care of it when he got here."

Confused, she shook her head. "Then why did you bring it?"

"Thought you might need one, considering the season and the occasion." He turned away, but before he vanished around the privacy panel, he paused and said, "Guess you still don't remember me, do you?"

Remember him? What did that mean?

Jess started to follow him around the panel and would've gone right up to the door, knocking, demanding to know what he meant, except that she couldn't. Her feet carried her back the other way—inside and to the photo album.

She touched the leather cover. Like a faint whisper in her head, she heard a name.

Drew.

She lifted the cover of the beach album, but stopped short of opening it. The pictures played out in her head instead.

Kids on the beach. Shorts and sweat jackets. The smell of salt and ocean. Squeals and shouts.

Drew. His last name tarried at the fringes of her memory. She'd remember when she wasn't trying. That's how those things worked.

She hadn't recognized him. Hardly surprising. She hadn't forgotten him. It had been long ago, true, and brief, but some things don't get forgotten unless...

Unless one wanted to forget?

Jess closed her eyes and tried to recall his face, then and now. The dark eyes hadn't changed, or not much. The face had hardened, the bone structure stronger.

He'd been a cute kid. He'd seemed especially cute that last year when they were twelve.

Jess opened the album and thumbed through. He was in the group of kids on the beach. Suddenly, he was very clear and real in her head.

She looked toward the front door. He was only yards away. A few steps and a knock on the door, and then what? Trading old memories? How hypocritical could she be? Acting as though the memories meant something when she'd dismissed him from her life so easily?

A few steps away. Next door. She had to say something.

Maybe an acknowledgement then? He'd arrived with that tree and a foolish smile on his face. He'd remembered the Dawson's and had brought an evergreen welcome in his arms. So an acknowledgement from her, and maybe an apology, too,

45

was called for.

Before going outside, she stopped to fill a large cup with water and poured it into the basin of the tree stand. Someone else had done that when the tree was outside and she was pretty sure she knew who—someone who'd tried to keep the tree fresh during its stay on the porch.

Jess stepped outside, but didn't make it past her side of the privacy panel. Pete walked up the steps to the porch.

"Jessie." He stood on the crossover, not moving onto the porch itself. He wore a cap. Water droplets covered it. The sleeves of his jacket were wet.

A few raindrops sprinkled them as they stood there. Her jaw tightened. Annoyance spurred aggression. Those feelings rose in her, battling for prominence.

A small voice in her brain told her to back off. She crossed her arms, in fact, holding them. It might appear to be a stubborn pose, but it also kept her hands from wringing his neck.

"Lila's not here," she said.

"I know." He looked down at his shoes, then up again. He met her eyes. "I want to speak with you."

"Why? Whatever is going on between you and Lila isn't my business and you don't need my approval."

"Not really true, though."

"So you care what I think?" She scoffed. Not likely.

He shrugged. "Not really, except for how it affects Lila. She cares a lot."

"Since when?" Jess threw the words out in reflex and heard the sharpness in them. She jammed her hands into her pockets.

Pete frowned. He opened his mouth, then closed it again. Finally he said, "You really don't know? Or do you not care?"

"Not care? I love my sister. What is it that you think I don't care about?"

"I don't believe you understand that she cares what you think. The stuff you do, the things you say, hurt her."

Her chest grew tight. "We all get hurt some time or other."

He asked, "What did I ever do to you?"

"To me?"

Pete looked at his shoes. "If I ever gave you reason to think..."

"No. Don't even go there. That has nothing to do with anything. Nothing. My only concern is my sister." Jess moved closer to the crossover, her fingers twitching in her pockets, the nails digging into her palms. "Lila has never asked for my approval for any man she's dated, so I keep my opinions to myself, but I see the stress that dating you causes her. The anxiety. I know something about that personally, don't I?"

"I know she cries. I don't think it's because of me or anything I do."

Pete's hands were in his pockets, too. His face was flushed despite the chill and the rain. Jess examined him as if inspecting a dead insect. His shoulders drooped and he looked away.

He said, "She cries when she talks about you."

Jess turned away. She'd heard enough.

She hadn't forced her opinions on Lila, but she hadn't been hypocritical either. She never pretended to feel other than she did. She was honest. Always.

"I want to ask a favor. You don't have to like me, or even go out of your way to be nice to me. I guess I can't even blame you. But for Lila…for Lila could you try a little kindness?"

Pete left, and Jess had little taste for speaking to anyone else. This seemed an ill-fated day for personal interactions. Not that it was her fault. She hadn't done anything wrong, but she wasn't a kid either. By this age, she should know how to finesse dialogue and not use it like a baseball bat.

She didn't want Pete back. There hadn't been anything between them *worth* wanting, only the potential for it. Sometimes the potential was more attractive than what reality delivered. But that didn't mean she thought Pete was right for her sister.

Jess vowed to stop worrying about Lila. She'd made her choice for companionship and it wasn't her big sister.

She went back inside. The photo album was lying open on the table and the photographs caught her eye again. Drew was in many of them.

She sat and rested her cheek against her hand.

There he was, a tall, thin boy on the beach with Rob or looking at a seashell with her, even posing with Rob and Dad, cozy on the steps while she leaned on the railing nearby.

Yet, she had forgotten. Not him, but instead the memories that should've been very important to her. How did that happen?

****

Jess steeled herself to knock on his door. He didn't answer. She was glad.

She sat at the end of the crossover, her legs curled up under her, observing the damp sand, the ocean which seemed calmer now, and the heavy, low clouds that had absorbed all of the color and blotted the brightness from the day. Almost one color, one tone. One shade of gray. She filled her brain with the view and her senses with the salty sting of the ocean breeze and the wet chill of the air, and kept every other thought at bay.

Winter's early darkness was descending even earlier because of the clouds.

She unwrapped her limbs and stood, gingerly getting the blood flow restored to her legs. Would she knock on his door again?

No. She'd sat here in plain view for an hour. Judging by his past behavior, he would've seen her if he was in the duplex and would've come out to speak if he'd felt so inclined. He'd been angry though, that last time, so maybe he was done with it.

Jess bypassed his door and went inside.

~ Two Days 'til Christmas ~

Jess spent the night on the sofa, though not intentionally. She'd fallen asleep while reading a book. The book was resting on her face when she woke and likely was far better rested than she.

She stretched to work the kinks out of her back and neck. A hot shower resolved the last of it. Unlike yesterday, today truly would be a better day. As soon as she went back downstairs and had a bite of breakfast, she'd call Rob.

She visualized it—his family recovered and on their way. She'd bring out the presents and the boxes of tree decorations she'd brought with her, the special ornaments they all remembered, and jump back into holiday mode.

Jess descended the stairs with a lighter step.

Lila's bags were gathered into a pile on the floor. Lila emerged from the closet with her coat. She glanced at Jess, then looked away and kept moving.

"I came back to get my stuff. I put the key on the kitchen counter."

"Really? Is this necessary?" Jess walked over to the pile. "Where are you staying?"

"Don't worry about it. We're fine."

"You and Pete, you mean."

"Sure."

"He came by yesterday afternoon a few hours after

you two left. Did you know?"

Lila kept moving. She picked up two bags.

"He asked me to be nicer to you. I'd rather have heard it from you directly. But then you didn't tell me Pete was bringing coffee to you yesterday morning, either. You pretended not to know he was coming."

"I didn't pretend. I didn't know. I was talking to him on the phone and mentioned coffee. I didn't know he was down here. He wanted to surprise me."

"Well, he did. So tell me the truth. Do you think I'm harsh? Unfair?"

Lila's eyes darkened, or maybe it was the narrowing of her eyes, the lowering of her long-lashed eyelids that created the effect.

"Yes."

She drew in a rough breath. "I'm not perfect, but I'm not unfair."

Lila stared at her.

"Fine. Tell me when." Jess waved her hands. "Come on, give me a for instance."

"Okay. For instance, it wasn't my fault."

"About Pete? He and I–"

"No, not about Pete."

"What then?"

Lila dropped the bags near the door. She reached for her scarf, then paused. "In fact, you didn't seem to care all that much about Pete. Seemed like you forgot him pretty easily, that is, until daddy died."

Jess shook her head. "One doesn't have anything to do with the other."

"Except that Pete came to the funeral, and he and I got to know each other. Suddenly, you were outraged. About him being around? Or for being with me? I don't know. But it's more than that. You blame me for our father's death."

Stunned, breathless, as if she'd been punched in the stomach, Jess searched for words. "Why would you say that? Why would that even cross your mind?"

"Don't pretend."

"Pretend what? Say it. Speak it out loud. Let's get this over with now."

Lila pointed at her. "You always resented me. I was spoiled, right? The baby of the family. How many times did I hear you telling Mom and Dad to be harder on me? You were…"

"You've gone this far. Say the rest."

"You were jealous."

Jess's throat was tight. She reached up to with one hand to press against it, trying to break the hold that was strangling her.

Lila said, "Okay, maybe not jealous, but you resented me."

Jess shook and took a deep breath. "I resented what you put them through."

"I was a teenager. They understood."

"They worried. And then you left."

"Left? I went to college."

"Out of state," Jess said. "Might as well have been out of the country for all the trips you didn't make home for the holidays."

"I graduated at the top of my class. I wasn't fooling around up in Boston, you know that. And I worked besides."

Then grad school, Jess thought, though she didn't say it aloud. Plus, after she earned her degrees, Lila had found a great job.

Jess shook her head. "Never mind. You didn't do anything wrong."

"You say that, but you still blame me for that and more." Lila gave a rough, low scream. "For heaven's sake, Jess. You let your husband move away without you rather than leave our parents. Ex-husband, that is. No one asked you to do something like that. You let him go, and Pete, too. Those were your choices."

"Easy for you to say. Our brother had just married and moved out of town. You remember how Mama cried."

"Yes, but she was supposed to be sad. It was a happy sad. A good sad."

Jess continued as if there'd been no response. "And you were about to leave for college. When Mama had that cancer scare, at about the same time that Matthew said he'd accepted the transfer to Phoenix, I weighed my choices and decided not to go. It wasn't only about our parents. You know Matthew and I had issues."

Lila shouted, "But I did come home, didn't I? I found a new job and moved back here to be near family, then Dad died. That gave you one more thing to add to your list, the list of all the terrible things I've done."

Jess turned away.

"Each time I screwed up or something wasn't perfect, it was one more mark against me, but what you're really angry about, what you hold against me, isn't leaving, and isn't Pete. It's that if I hadn't moved back to town and bought that house, and if Dad hadn't come over to help me hang paper that day, he might not have had that heart attack."

"If you'd been there helping him, instead of out shopping, you could've called 9-1-1. It might've made a difference." She shook her head. "But it wasn't your fault. Accuse me of whatever you want, but not that. I never blamed you for losing Dad." Jess shook her head again. "Why on earth would you think that I did?"

Jess wanted to put her hands on her sister's shoulders, maybe on her face, her cheeks, and make her see through Jess's eyes and into her brain, into her heart. But there was also a part of Jess that wanted to bare her palms and slap Lila, maybe push her. The thought of even being able to imagine doing any kind of violence to her sister horrified her. Could there be a germ of truth in what Lila said? Not jealousy, but resentment? Maybe. Jess wasn't convinced either way, so she kept her arms tightly crossed.

Jess asked, "Does this have anything to do with Pete? Has he been talking to you, putting these ideas into your head? He doesn't know a thing about what I'm thinking or feeling. Nothing. He should mind his own business."

Lila's eyes grew dark, large, overfilling with emotion.

Jess thought she'd gotten through to Lila. She relaxed her fists, feeling the fingers peel away from her palms, flexing. She wanted to hug her sister and apologize for the unintended put-downs, for their misunderstandings. She meant it, too, but didn't get to say the words.

"Typical. It's Pete's fault. Always someone else's fault. You want to control everyone. You never liked any of my boyfriends. You never give anyone new a chance, or anyone else a second chance."

Her words ripped through Jess, tearing at her. She threw sharp words back at Lila. "I don't want to control you or anyone else! I'm tired of trying to hold this family together." She waved her hands. "I quit. You can all go your own way. Everyone already has. Even my own mother. I quit. Do you hear me? Go to Pete. Leave me alone."

Lila yelled back, "You're in your thirties, Jess. You have another forty, maybe fifty years ahead of you. Do you really want to continue into the future this way? Not living your own life?"

Jess snagged her jacket from the chair by the door as Lila added, "You're so full of everyone else's life you have no room for your own."

She fled, leaving Lila standing there, the last words barely off her lips.

She ran along the crossover, stumbled down the steps and through the drifts of dry sand, then half-ran up the beach. She misjudged a wave and one sneaker got soaked. The sand worked in around her ankle and rubbed between skin and shoe like sand paper. Miserable. It slowed her down to a limp.

She was angry. She was embarrassed. She quit.

She needed to quit, apparently, for everyone's sake, including her own.

Jess sat on the sand and dug the worst of the sand out from between her shoe and ankle. She leaned forward, arms extended across her knees, and put her head down, hiding her face, rejecting the sun.

"Are you sick or meditating or what?"

The tips of his shoes in the sand were visible through that small, triangular window formed by her arm, thigh and mid-section. She didn't look up.

Her intrusive neighbor. Her tree delivery guy. And more. Always showing up unexpectedly. Funny how his voice, his manner, now that she remembered him, were so familiar.

She lifted her head, but stared across the ocean at the horizon. A sea-going vessel of some kind was out there. It was too distant to make out details and she didn't know much about such things anyway. Still, she was a little envious. That ship was going somewhere. Somewhere that wasn't here.

"I'm okay. Just hanging out."

"Sounds like you want to be alone."

Jess shrugged and nodded.

"I saw you go by. I wasn't spying, but that door closed pretty hard. The house shook a little. Got my attention."

"My sister and I had a disagreement."

"Happens."

Stupid remark, but the casual ordinariness of it, the truth of it, sort of a universal truth of brothers and sisters, reoriented her.

"You're right." She dropped her arms to her side and sat up straighter. "Sorry we disturbed you."

"No problem. It's hard on the door though. Let me know if it needs any work. I'm handy that way."

She refused to warm to his pathetic humor. The silence grew a tad uncomfortable. She let it draw out to show she didn't need his sympathy.

"Well, I'll head back then," he said.

"Sure. Thanks." Inwardly, Jess groaned. She called out. "Wait. Please."

She stood and brushed the sand from her slacks. Now that she recognized him, and remembered, she couldn't ignore or dismiss him. She had to say something, to acknowledge the truth.

"I do remember you."

He made a non-committal noise.

Jess said, "It's been a long time. How'd you know anyway?"

"Know what?"

"That the Dawson's were returning to Emerald Isle and Coral Cove for Christmas. I doubt you've been bringing a tree every year, just in case we showed up, so, yeah, how'd you know?"

"You're sarcastic."

"Cynical, I guess."

"Or maybe the opposite."

Too tender? If that's what he meant, perhaps he was right. "That's not what we're talking about."

"I saw the family name when the house was rented." He shrugged. "Had to be the same Dawson's."

"You could've said something sooner."

"That was the plan. Didn't know what I was walking into. Had a crazy idea that some of you might remember me on your own."

She had more than one memory of him, and more than one apology was owed for a wrong done long ago. He'd probably forgotten about it before summer was past, maybe even before the dust settled behind their tires. They were kids back then, after all. No reason for him to hold a grudge.

Jess felt guilty anyway. She tried to think of how to express it, but chickened out. How much did it matter, really?

She shifted her stance. "I'd better get inside. See if Rob has called."

"If you need a hand with that tree, or the door, you let me know."

He started walking away. Leaving.

She could do the same. Pack up and go home. Walk away from this whole botched holiday non-event. But now quite yet.

"Wait," she said.

He stopped.

"I doubt I'll be back here. Ever. There's something I'd like to say."

He tilted his head. "Yeah?"

"I owe you an apology." Inside, Jess cringed. She was going to say it.

"No worries."

"No, I mean I really do. I've owed it for a long time."

"I don't understand."

"I do remember you and I'm sorry you had to remind me."

"You don't owe me an apology for that. It's been way too long to even want to count the years."

"No, that's not the apology I meant." Jess walked slowly along the sand and Drew joined her and kept pace. "That last Christmas we were down here, I accused you of stealing. I told my parents you'd stolen Rob's wallet."

"It was a long time ago. I'd forgotten."

"Did you?"

"Long time gone. Besides, it wasn't an intentional lie. You thought I had. You were mistaken."

"That's it, you see. I really was mistaken." The image of the sand below the far end of the porch popped into her head. "When we were leaving, I saw it in the sand. It must've fallen off the porch. It was mostly covered by sand. I didn't tell anyone. I left it there."

"Did you? Why?"

Jess shrugged and shook her head. "I was embarrassed."

"You didn't like to be wrong even back then."

"Again, I'm sorry."

Should she be more embarrassed about something she'd done years ago or over the fact that she'd so easily packed the memory away and put it out of her mind?

"Are you limping?" he asked.

"What? Oh, I'm fine." She shook her foot. "Sand in my shoe, that's all."

"You could take your shoe off and–" He reached toward her.

"I'm fine, I said."

"Sure. Okay. You might regret it later, though." He shrugged. "So back to your apology. Don't worry about it. I don't blame you. I don't think you liked me, well, sort of moving in on your family group." He looked at the high, thin white clouds moving across the blue sky. "Plus, you were mad at me for another reason."

Jess didn't want to talk about that, but the least she could do was stand in silence and give him a chance to have his say. She shifted position. Her feet were cold.

But he didn't pursue the thought. Instead, he moved on. "So. What should we do about it? You want to go tell my mom, or what? Get me out of trouble?"

Jess didn't need to see his face. She heard the lilt in his voice. She was off the guilt hook that easily? She tried to match his light, joking attitude.

"I guess I'm the only one who cares?"

"Hey, I was the one who was grounded. I think I'm owed something for that at least.

She tucked her hair behind her ear and looked at

him sort of sideways. "What did you have in mind?"

"It's been a quarter of a century. Give me some time to think about it."

"As you wish," she said.

His voice dropped and he stared at a seabird flying by. "Besides, I don't think you were angry so much about me being around as because..."

So he wanted to say it aloud after all.

"You don't need to toy with me."

"I think I do." He grinned. "The way I remember it, you tried to kiss me."

"Alright, I'm humiliated. Then and now. You have your revenge. Satisfied?"

He didn't answer. He moved on as if the conversation had never gone there.

Jess was both annoyed and embarrassed. He'd given the memory life by speaking the words, but was now dropping the subject, unfinished, as if it didn't matter at all. She bit her lip.

"I wish I could've said hello to your mom when she stopped by. I didn't want to intrude. I thought I'd have time. I remember her. Very nice lady. I remember your father, too."

"He's gone. Almost a year."

"I'm sorry. He was a great dad, I mean, what little I knew of him. Your parents were kind. It would get so quiet here in the winter. It was...compelling...magnetic to have other kids so close in age to me nearby. I'm sure I was a pest, but they never made me feel that way."

"Heart attack."

Drew nodded.

"Totally unexpected. Probably would've survived it if he'd received medical help right away."

"But?"

"He was hanging wallpaper. Like he was still a teenager or something."

"Like a teenager?"

"You know what I mean. He wasn't a kid and shouldn't have been up on that ladder."

"I assume that's what he enjoyed, wanted to do."

"He did it because my sister had moved into a new house and asked him to help. And if he hadn't been left alone while she went shopping…. It doesn't matter now. What's done is done."

"So it's all over except the forgiveness?"

She put her hands over her face, then through her hair. "You overheard Lila."

"Yep, you Dawson's are loud people. She was a baby when I knew her. Cute kid, as I recall."

"The baby of the family. Where do you get off lecturing me about forgiveness?"

"I forgave you."

"For something I did as a kid many years ago."

"You are so…touchy. Worse than I remember." He kicked at the sand. "So what about Rob? I was looking forward to saying hello. I bet he'll remember me even though some people didn't."

"His kids are sick."

"They do that. Too bad. Well, maybe next year."

"There won't be another year. This is the last."

Her fingers were chilly. Jess put her hands in her pockets. "My sister is angry because she says I blame her for our father's death."

"Do you?"

"I can't imagine how she'd even come up with that. I guess some people feel better about themselves by putting the fault on others."

"Do you blame her?"

"No, I don't." She cringed at the strident tone in her voice. She tried again. "I don't."

"I believe you."

"Nice of you."

"No, seriously. You wouldn't be the first person to hold a loved one's death against someone else whether it made sense or not. People get crazy when it comes to grief. Did you tell her?"

"I did. I'm pretty sure she didn't believe me." Her voice drifted off across the ocean. She said louder, "She doesn't believe me."

"You're tough on her sometimes?"

"Tough? Please." Jess laughed, but not happily. "Why am I even talking to you? You don't know me. We aren't friends. Not even acquaintances. I knew you, what? For a few days twenty-five years ago? How could you understand how I feel about anything?"

"I don't have any siblings and I'm still single. I don't know anything about anything."

"Well, you're certainly very free with your judgments and your opinions."

"I am."

A chill breeze brushed past, touched her face. "My cheeks are cold. I should've brought a scarf or mittens."

"Want my coat?"

"You're just giving me a hard time, aren't you?

Drew said, "Somebody has to."

"What's that supposed to mean?"

"I haven't seen you in twenty-five years, at least not until a few days ago, but you haven't changed."

The amusement in his voice was unmistakable.

"That's ridiculous. I can't imagine why I'm talking to you. You know nothing about me."

"I know you rented a house and invited your whole family and the only ones who showed up took off almost as quickly as they arrived."

Her chest went tight. She dragged the air into her lungs, then forced the words out. "I love my family."

"No doubt about that."

Words failed her. She turned away.

"I'm sorry. I went too far." He touched her shoulder.

She shook his hand off.

"This was stupid of me. Again, I'm sorry. I'll leave you alone." He started to walk away.

Jess called after him, "I do everything I can for them. Everything. I'd give up anything for them."

He stopped and turned around. He came back only a step or two. "What about you?"

"About me?"

"Giving up your life, I mean."

"I have a great life. A great house. Excellent job. I do very well, thank you."

"Not what I meant."

"Are you asking if I got married? Marriage isn't everything, you know, but yes, I did. Right out of high school. It didn't last. We didn't value the same things. Even so, we parted well. My life has been great."

"Great."

"That's right. Great."

"Yeah, I meant…that's what I meant. It's great you have a good life."

"Why am I being cross-examined anyway? What about your life?"

He shrugged. "No secrets. Not much to say."

"Well, then," Jess said with all the spite she could dredge up. "Maybe that's why you're so interested in mine."

"Actually, I was a little interested given the past, but you're the one who invited me into your family affairs. You brought up blaming your sister for your father's death, not me."

"I don't blame her."

"I believe you."

"Alright. Fair is fair. You've made me feel terrible. Tell me something bad about yourself."

"Bad?"

"Really bad." She sounded about ten years old. Correction, twelve. "Really, really bad."

"Like prison time, maybe?"

Her heart stilled. It had the effect of cooling the worst of her temper. She would never intentionally demean anyone, or put them in the position where they would do it to themselves. She should apologize. Before she could, he spoke again.

Drew added, "Not that I've been to prison, but is that the kind of thing you were hoping to hear?"

Her feet were suddenly getting very cold. Her ire had diminished and she didn't want to play this childish game any longer.

"No, I'm done. You win. Whatever it was you were after, you win." Jess walked past, keeping plenty of distance between them.

"I live with my mother."

Huh? She couldn't help herself. He was the feather and she was the fascinated cat.

"What?"

"Sure. No self-respecting man my age would want a woman to know that. Or anyone to know, for that matter. You could embarrass me."

She shook her head. She felt inside-out and twisted around. Never in her life could she remember a time when she felt her world was this upside down and whirling to boot. Not even when she let her marriage die.

"It's kind of like neither of us left home," he said.

Jess shivered. "I'm exhausted. Next time don't be so helpful, okay? I might not survive it."

She stumbled through the dry sand, abandoning the last of her pride wanting only to escape.

Drew called out, "Hey, my mom's cooking tonight. She's pretty good. I'll pick you up at five p.m."

"No thanks."

"You owe me, remember? You can confess and get me off the hook. Might even change the course of my wayward life."

Confess? Oh, he meant she could confess to his mother about the lie she'd told. Whatever.

"Sure." Her head was spinning. Dinner at five with his mom? Somehow it seemed like the least she could do to atone.

****

For the Dawson children, Drew had been a sort of disembodied kid—no past, no future—a local. In some ways, he was greatly to be envied because he was a local and this was Emerald Isle, the beach. What a fantastic place to be 'local.' But their relationship was short-term, finite, not like social interactions in a neighborhood or church or school that grow over time. He was a local kid and they were vacationers.

The Dawson's were also a family unit. A solid core. Team Dawson. Any extraneous attachments were easily left behind upon departure for home.

So now, many years later, having been reminded that he had, indeed, existed, and that she'd tried to kiss him—no more than an innocent peck on the cheek, of course—and he'd embarrassed her and then she'd accused him of stealing...

Young love had its hiccups. Maybe it was no wonder she'd put Drew, along with her own bad behavior, out of her mind.

Jess assumed dinner was casual. She took her hat and scarf thinking she might need them for the drive or the walk. She had no idea how close he lived, but when he was a kid, it must've have been fairly nearby since he'd hung around here during the day, every day.

He knocked on the door at five p.m. sharp. Jess greeted him, took pains to make sure she had her purse and jacket and to lock up, and he led her next door.

"Your mother's here?" She paused before crossing the threshold. "You said we were having dinner with her."

He cleared his throat with a small cough. "I said my mother was cooking."

Jess frowned. "Is this some kind of trick?"

Drew started to answer, but was stopped when the door opened wide. A thin, petite woman asked, "Are you two coming in or not?"

He ushered her inside. Jess breathed deeply. She looked at the woman and asked, "What's that?"

"Smothered pork chops. Hope you like pork?"

"I do." Whatever she'd smothered it with smelled heavenly.

Her hair was a faded, silvery blonde. "When Drew told me we were having company for dinner, I went through the freezer. Just happened I had enough of the pork chops to go around."

"Lucky me, I'd say." She smiled and extended her hand. "I'm Jessie Dawson. Please call me Jess."

"Pleased to meet you. Call me Kathy. Take your jacket off and make yourself cozy. I'll get back to the kitchen."

"What can I do?" Jess looked around. "May I set the table?"

"No need."

Jess ignored Drew and followed his mother into the kitchen. "I'm more of a doer than a sitter. Please, I'd like to help."

"Plates are on the counter. Silverware's in the drawer."

This side of the duplex was a mirror image of her side. The furnishings, the room arrangements, were similar, but flipped.

"Looks familiar over here," she joked.

"It's okay," Kathy said, as they carried the food to the table. "It's convenient for a meal, but I wouldn't want to live here."

"You came over just to cook?"

Kathy arranged the food dishes. "My kitchen is being renovated. Besides, there's no sense it letting these units stay idle. Appliances, like houses, don't do well unused."

Jess sat across from Drew and adjacent to Kathy. A few bites into the meal, she resumed the topic.

"You mentioned your kitchen was being renovated?" She focused on Kathy, deliberately avoiding eye contact with Drew. "Drew said he lives with you?"

Kathy sat back a fraction. Jess thought she'd hit some kind of nerve. She'd overstepped.

An instant of confusion registered on Kathy's face, then smoothed out and she smiled. "Well, goodness. He does...but it's more accurate to say I live with him. I had to retire because of health problems, but couldn't afford to, if you know what I mean?" She shook her head. "You're too young to have experienced that. Anyway, Drew invited me to live with him."

"That's very nice."

"Nicer than you might guess since he already had his sister's children living with him. But that's just how he is. He's a good and generous man. I'm a fortunate mom."

Drew said, "Enough. You work harder now raising your three grandchildren than at any of those jobs you had."

"It's a different kind of work. Not work, in fact."

"You did us the favor."

Jess was warmed by their words. "Three?"

Kathy smiled. "They are the best three kids in the world. No offense, if you have some of your own."

Jess shook her head. "Nieces and a nephew. My brother's children. I love them dearly, but they don't live with me."

"It's no wonder my son comes over here to work when the place isn't rented. It's the only peace he can find."

"What kind of work? I thought he was renovating or painting or fixing the plumbing or something?"

"Drew?" Kathy put her head back and laughed.

68

"No. During the off-season when the unit isn't rented much, he comes over here to work on accounts."

"Okay, mom. That's enough about me."

Drew was uncomfortable. Seeing that, Jess was tempted to tease him as he'd teased her earlier, but his mom was sweet and might not understand.

Kathy said, "Drew mentioned your family is, or was, coming down for Christmas? He was telling me about it, but then it sounded like it changed?"

"Life has a way of changing plans, I guess. The children came down sick, and so on. Life is unpredictable. Life with kids is even more so."

"That's certainly true."

During a quiet pause in the conversation, Jess cast a quick look at Drew. He raised his eyebrows in a question. Now was the time.

"Kathy, I have a confession to make, and an apology."

She asked, "To whom?"

"To you. I already apologized to Drew."

She frowned. "Really? About what?"

"Back when we were kids, when we came here for Christmas…it was the last year we came…there was a misunderstanding. I thought Drew had taken something and told my parents. I found out later that he didn't, but I never set the record straight."

Kathy's eyes had grown wide. She was attentive but clearly puzzled.

"My father spoke to you about it?"

"Honey. I 'm sorry. I don't remember it, but I'm glad it all got figured out."

Atonement for something the person didn't remember felt pointless, unfinished, or foolish. Jess felt

GRACE GREENE

foolish.

Drew was no help. He was already picking up the dirty dishes. Was he grinning?

Kathy patted her hand. "Aw, honey, don't worry about it."

As Kathy was speaking, Drew returned for more dishes and then Jess heard water running in the kitchen.

His mother patted her hand. "We all do stuff as kids that we regret, but kids have no sense of proportion, of judging how actions fit across the broader context. Probably felt like a big deal at the time. Sometimes that out-of-whack perception follows us into adulthood if we don't get it resolved. Nice that you had the chance to say you were sorry. Most never do. Could you pass that last roll before Drew runs off with the bread basket?"

Jess gave her the basket and also the butter dish. She was quiet, thinking about Kathy's words.

"Do you have plans for Christmas?" Kathy asked.

Her question brought Jess back to the present.

"I'm not sure. At this point, I'm thinking of packing up and driving home tomorrow. Maybe a change of plan will change my luck."

Drew stopped in the kitchen doorway, but didn't speak.

Kathy said, "I'm sorry it's come to that for you. I don't know if that's wise, though, to travel I-95 on Christmas Eve. The interstates are usually jammed, and there's weather coming through tomorrow."

"Weather?"

"Some precipitation, but early, I think. It may be cold enough to freeze."

"Don't worry. I'll check the forecast before heading home."

"We visit family in Raleigh on Christmas Eve and stay over, but we know alternate routes. Ways around the traffic. My sister Jenna and her husband live there. I'm sure they'd be happy to have you too."

Kathy's expression was sincere. Somehow, Jess doubted they'd welcome her, but even if they did, she preferred to be alone for Christmas than among strangers and, in a really sad way, she was going to get her wish.

Regardless of fault or intention, if she stayed at the beach house for Christmas, she'd be there alone. She didn't want that.

"Look at the time. I'd better get home." Kathy scooted her chair back. "I'm sorry about eating so early, but Mike is only fourteen. We like to give him the chance to learn responsibility and to earn a little cash by babysitting, but he's young and sometimes his sisters take advantage."

"It was a pleasure to meet you, Kathy."

"And you, too, dear. I hope you'll come back and see us again. Remember, the offer for Christmas Eve is open."

Drew escorted Jess the ten steps home. They were slow steps. Neither of them were in a hurry. Even so, it wasn't far enough. There was no time for her to ease questions into the general post-evening chit-chat, so she simply asked him.

"Accounts? What kind of accounts?"

"Bookkeeping types of accounts. I free-lance for local businesses, plus we have some business interests of our own." He knocked on the side of the house. "Like this."

"You're kidding? I'm staying at your house?"

He shrugged. "In a manner of speaking, you are."

Jess shook her head. "You know a lot about me. What about you? You never married? Seems unlikely."

"Because of my looks and charm?" He smiled at her, his face lit by the door light.

"Not so much, but your wit is definitely attention-getting."

He looked up at the stars, and then at the dark horizon. "I thought I would. Wanted to. But the ladies would get close, find out about my ready-made family, and the romance vanished."

"How did you end up with your sister's children?"

This time he looked down at his feet. He leaned back against the door and his expression turned wistful.

"She was my big sister."

"Was."

"Yep. Was. Her husband left. She and the kids moved in. I'm not some kind of saint. I never intended for them to stay. But June got sick and by then Mom's health was failing. Mom got better. We lost June."

Jess, sympathetic and moved by the truths they'd shared, ran her hand along his sleeve. Drew reached over and placed his hand on hers and held it there.

Gently, she eased her hand from his and touched his cheek. She said, "Your mom is delightful. Thanks for inviting me and I forgive you for making me confess for no reason."

Actually, in an ironic way kind of way she meant it. Something she hadn't realized was on her conscience, was now off of it. It felt okay to think about him, to remember him now. This self-revelation seemed to support what Kathy had said.

Jess was glad she was leaving with this unfinished

business resolved. It was an unexpected gift. Unfortunately, she was also taking a sad acceptance with her, too, when it came to her family.

It was time to move on with her own life.

~ Christmas Eve ~

Christmas Eve morning.

She'd stayed up late the evening before, stripping the unused beds and stashing the sheets in the bags provided by the rental agency. She gathered together most of her personal items in the bedroom and bathroom and then packed what she wouldn't need for the morning.

She left boxing up the food and decorations for this morning. She groaned aloud thinking about the trips she'd be making up and down those stairs.

Taking down the decorations could wait until last. Some insane, illogical sliver of hope lingered in her heart. She accepted it and moved on with what needed to be done.

The tree in the middle of the living room was living out her apparently prophetic statement—that she had no use for it. Not this year.

Jess opened the blinds.

The world was encrusted with diamonds.

They hung like flashing pendants from the porch railing. They sparkled on the floor planks and the crossover.

She opened the door and stepped out. Even the sand glittered. The dunes grasses were laid low under their shimmering coating. As she stood there another spate of ice was loosed from the sky.

It was sort of a white Christmas or at least a crystalline Christmas Eve morning.

Drew looked around the end of privacy panel. "You're still here. I'm glad."

"Good morning." Without thinking she stepped forward and her shoe hit where the ice began. She flailed, grabbing for the panel. Drew caught her arms.

He said, "No driving this morning."

"No, I guess not. It's beautiful. Exquisite."

Suddenly, the clouds parted and the sun poured forth in bright streams. She shielded her eyes, nearly blinded. Every surface, every faceted plane reflected the sun's rays.

"No," she said. "It's breathtaking."

"It is."

She peeked between her fingers and saw that his eyes were on her face.

He cleared his throat and added, "Storm's done. The ice won't last long. If you don't mind a later start, you can still get going today."

Oddly disappointed, Jess said, "I guess I could." She dropped her hands despite the brightness.

Why was she leaving anyway? What was the point in rushing back? It would be a quiet Christmas. A lonely one. Big deal. She'd better get used to lonely holidays. That said, she was never going to put herself through anything like this again. The bigger the expectations, the harder the crash.

She squinted at Drew. "What are you doing tomorrow?"

"Christmas Day?"

"Yeah."

"Mom and the kids are going over to Raleigh later

today when the ice clears up. I think she mentioned it to you at supper last night? I considered driving over too—I usually do—but I don't think I will this year. Aunt Jenna will have a full house. I'd like a quieter Christmas. So, the answer is I don't think I have any plans."

"Would you care to share Christmas dinner with me?"

"Yeah?" His dark eyes picked up the light from the ice and sparkled. He seemed surprised and pleased.

Encouraged, she repeated the invitation with a little joke.

"Sure. You'll have more opportunities to torture me." She fastened her eyes on his. "Seriously, I have tenderloin and it's not frozen. It needs to be cooked and eaten. I think we're up to the task."

"What about this evening?"

"What about it?" she asked.

"I'm alone this evening, too."

"Well, I'm not surprised. You're very pushy."

"I am. I practice it."

"So what did you have in mind?"

****

Drew arrived with takeout.

General Tso's chicken, rice and spring rolls for Christmas Eve dinner? Felt wrong. Even a bit daring. Definitely not traditional. But then, Jess reminded herself, the meal fit right in with the rest of the holiday this year—nothing had gone as usual or as planned.

She gathered plates, silverware and napkins.

"It's takeout," Drew said.

Jess turned to face him, the place settings in her hands.

"The point is not to have to wash dishes."

She looked down at the plates, then back at Drew. "I don't understand. We need plates and utensils."

He reached into the bag and drew out paper-wrapped chopsticks. He waved them at the white boxes.

"I don't know how to use those."

"I'll teach you."

They compromised on the plates. Jess tried the chopsticks but finally fetched herself a fork.

They had about five minutes of laughing and being friendly, then somewhere between the chopsticks and spring rolls something shifted. He smiled, that same smile she'd seen many times over the last few days, but this time it was sweeter and the lines at the corners of his eyes were more endearing. Jess became so acutely aware of him that she briefly lost the ability to speak. She focused on eating and avoiding his gaze and keeping her breathing even.

While they were eating, he saw the ornament box sitting next to the tree and stared at it for a few seconds. He finished his food and she thought he'd forgotten it. He stood and walked over to it. He picked the box up and rummaged through the contents. He brought out an ornament.

"This was mine. My favorite." He sat the box on the sofa and held up the ornament to show her.

"Really?" Jess examined it. It was bell-shaped and scratched up. "Why?"

He reached out and bent the ornament's wire hook over a branch.

"I know it's old. Used. It's still my favorite." After a quick glance over at her, he selected another ornament from the box.

"I meant, why would you leave your box of ornaments on the porch if they were so special to you?"

"Thought you might need them. With three kids and a grandmother in the house for several years, we have more ornaments, mostly handmade, than we can ever use. The tree is loaded."

His words reminded Jess of their tree when she was a child. It had been the same. The ornaments crafted by little fingers ended up thickly hung in that evergreen region about three feet above the floor. Her parents would casually, judiciously, distribute them more evenly on the tree in such a way that the kids felt like they'd directed the final, perfect arrangements. So long ago.

"I could put some Christmas music on." Lame, but she didn't know what else to say.

"I like the quiet," Drew said, digging out a frosted red ball.

"The tree is in the middle of the floor. Shouldn't we move it first?"

"I think the tree is great right here. Nice that it's not stuck in the corner."

She wasn't sure he was being honest about that but, for once in her life, she was enjoying going along, not having to be in charge.

"I'll be right back," she said.

Jess went the bedroom where she'd left the boxes, including the boxes holding the wrapped presents. The "Don't Open 'til Christmas" stickers had proved superfluous.

She found the box she wanted and returned with it in her arms. She held it out to Drew.

"These are my favorites," she said.

He lifted the lid and set it aside. "Lots of 'em. Are you allowed more than one favorite?"

"I don't see why not."

"Well, if you insist on decorating the tree with all these, we'd better string the lights first."

Her insist? Really? This hadn't been her idea. Jess started to protest that he was the one who wanted to decorate the tree and that it was a lot of work for only one night.

"Something wrong?" he asked.

It hit her that they were both getting what they wanted, even if her own particular 'want' was a little murky to her.

"Not a thing. I'll find the extension cords."

As twilight fell and the colorful lights glowed, Jess and Drew decorated the tree. Jess realized the room had grown dark except for those tiny lights. Her hand stopped short of flipping the light switch and instead lit the holiday candles on the coffee table and counter. Mostly they worked in silence, only occasionally remarking on an ornament or a memory. It was like slow dancing in a magical bubble with movements so simple they were all the more intricate. It was over too soon.

The tree was done. Both boxes, his and hers, were empty of ornaments. Jess didn't want to move beyond that moment. If she didn't speak...

"We aren't done yet," he said, breaking the spell.

Breathless, she asked, "No?"

"There's no topper. A star or an angel?"

Jess looked up at the top of the tree. It was, indeed, empty. She shook her head, illogically embarrassed. "You're right. I guess I forgot to bring one."

Drew smiled. Jess wanted to touch his face, to trace

the line of his jaw and lips with her fingers, but she kept those wayward hands at bay.

"Time for me to go, I guess," he said.

She heard the question in his voice and she could've said no, but tomorrow would be a new day. She didn't want to mess it up by not saying goodbye tonight. Plus, she was more than a little apprehensive. She hadn't dated in a long time, not since Pete, and Pete hardly counted.

As she handed Drew his jacket, she took the opportunity to touch his sleeve. At the door they paused.

He said, "We have some unfinished business."

"What's that?"

"The kiss? The one that didn't go as planned?"

"Of course." Her voice came out as a whisper. "Do you want me to apologize for that, too?"

"No, in fact. It's my turn to apologize." He brushed her neck, her ear with his cupped hand, then lightly lifted her chin. "I was a little panicked at the time. You were a year older, you know."

"Eight months."

"Yes, an older woman. I was scared. I ran off."

"You left me standing there feeling stupid and embarrassed."

"Guilty as charged. I've practiced, though. I'm a much better kisser now."

"Really?"

He slid his arms around her and pulled her close, and proved it.

Drew was gone, but Jess was unwilling to extinguish what was left of the magical evening. She curled up on the sofa surrounded by the colorful and flickering lights and rested her head back against the cushion. She hugged a pillow and half-closed her eyes so that the colored lights became a kaleidoscope and the scene could've been any time, any Christmas.

From the recesses of her brain and memory, she heard her mother's voice, faint but unmistakable, calling them to gather around and settle down. The air swirled with the sharp scent of evergreen and the sweet aroma of cocoa.

So many Christmas Eves filled her memory. Year after year Dad had read aloud to them re-telling the angel Gabriel's message, the journey of Joseph and Mary from Nazareth to Bethlehem, of the birth of the Holy Child in the stable, and the visit of shepherds and wise men to welcome and honor Him.

Even now, alone at the beach house, she listened and heard the warm, sure sound of Dad's voice sharing the words. It felt real, and it was—as real now as it had ever been. Not everything had to be seen to be true. The heart could know what the eyes might not recognize or understand.

Jess rested her head on the pillow and sofa arm. Her spirit was at ease for the first time in a long time.

Gifts came in many ways and forms. Some were held close, some shared, but all were to be cherished.

~ Christmas Day ~

The tenderloin roast was huge. She'd purchased it when she thought she'd be cooking for eight and, as always, she allowed for extra helpings.

She set the rolls to rising and prepared the green salad. For only two, it made sense to limit the side dishes, so she settled for potatoes with au jus gravy, asparagus, and the salad. It was too early to start the actual cooking so she lined the items up on the counter, staging them for the real event, then went upstairs to finish getting herself ready.

It had been a long time since she'd been on a date. Yesterday didn't count. Nor did dinner with his mom. Well, maybe those counted as a launching point.

A little makeup was in order. Fluff the hair. Check the image in the mirror. Funny how the clothes one wore for self or family looked different when viewed from a dating perspective. Frumpy. Jess ditched the sweater vest with the jingle bells but kept on the burgundy knit top she wore beneath it. It was the best she could do with what she had.

She expected Drew to arrive at about one p.m. At eleven a.m. he called and asked if Kathy and the kids could come along.

"Sorry. Not quite what we'd planned. By the time the ice was clearing, my aunt called. My uncle has a stomach virus. Mom doesn't want to expose the kids."

Jess's first reaction wasn't her finest, but then she remembered the quantity of tenderloin. Plus, it wasn't long ago that she'd lamented the empty seats at her Thanksgiving table, and more recently, at the table here.

Find the upside. Having Drew's mom and the children join them for Christmas dinner wasn't part of the plan, but maybe their presence would liven things up and diminish any awkwardness she and Drew might feel. If this thing with Drew was worth building on, then his mom and kids were only a step, hopefully a helpful step, on the way.

"The more, the merrier," she said.

Knowing they wouldn't be alone took some of the edge from her nerves.

Some. When she passed the mirror, she stopped to check her hair again and saw she was grinning like an eager puppy about to be awarded a special treat.

The table was already set for two. She added four more places. The centerpiece was a simple arrangement of red and green tapered candles. She switched those out for the nutcracker soldier candles and added a few sprigs of garland entwined with candy canes to make it more festive for the children.

What was a person supposed to do with three kids? One could feed them. She knew how to do that.

Jess stood beside the table and laughed. She should blame Thanksgiving for this. A full table for Christmas dinner, yet not one of the guests was related to her. There was irony, or maybe a message, hidden in there.

She went back to cooking, but after a short while someone knocked on the side door. She looked at the clock. Drew wasn't due for an hour yet.

Jess grabbed a dish towel and dried her hands on

the way to the door.

Lila stood on the threshold. "Hi," she said. Her eyes were large and misty.

Jess was stunned. "I thought you'd left town."

"Started to. But."

"But."

"Is it too late to share some Christmas with you?"

Jess couldn't speak. Instead, she jumped forward and threw her arms around Lila.

"You okay, Jess?"

She nodded, sniffling. She released her and stepped back. "Come in."

Lila stopped just inside the room. "The tree. It's decorated."

"It is. In fact I had some help."

"Six plates?" She was staring at the table.

"Yes. I have something to tell you."

A frown crossed Lila's face. "Did Rob and the kids..."

"No. Last I heard from them they were still sick." She tried to remember when they'd last spoken? Early yesterday? Or the evening before that?

She needed another plate. "What about Pete?"

Lila shook her head. "He's driving back to Richmond. It's okay, Jess. He understands and I do, too. You're right. We'll work out whatever needs to be worked out after the holidays."

Jess almost felt guilty. Almost. She added a plate for Lila. That made seven. Close to perfect, really, in terms of filling up a table for a holiday meal.

"Will you give me a hand with the salad while I get the roast ready for the oven? The bowl's in the fridge."

Lila opened the door and looked inside. "Is this it?"

She stepped back, holding the bowl and eyeing it doubtfully.

"Yes, you can see there's not enough. I was making it for two."

"Two? Not six?"

"Yes, two. Can you add more salad? Enough for seven, and maybe a little extra?"

"Only if you tell me what's going on." Lila stared. "Are you blushing? You are. You're turning red."

Jess held up her hand. "Wait and I'll explain it all when we have a few quiet moments."

"In detail."

"Promise." She slid the roast into the oven, checking the time. "He should be here soon."

"He who?"

"Drew."

"Don't make me drag this from you piece by piece."

Jess laughed. Another knock. This time on the front door. Lila and she turned in unison and saw Drew through the glass.

"Him?"

"Him and others." Jess ran to let them in. "Welcome."

Drew held the door for his mother and the kids. Inside, Kathy patted the top of each head as she introduced them. "Mike, Lisa and Meg." Mike topped his grandmother by several inches so the loving gesture made Jess smile.

"Nice to meet you all."

"I told Drew it wasn't right to inconvenience you this way."

"Nonsense. I'm glad you're all here. No one wants

to sit down to an empty table at Christmas."

The youngest girl was shorter than Janie, but looked older than Suze. Her glossy curls were gathered back with a red ribbon. She was holding something in her small hands.

Drew touched her hair. "Meggie brought this for the tree."

"An angel. We needed one." Jess dabbed at her eyes that were suddenly teary. Her vision was a little blurry.

Meggie smiled shyly and held out the homemade angel. Drew put his hands around her waist and lifted her high enough to reach the top. Mike automatically put out a hand to steady the tree.

Lila said. "It's beautiful."

Jess smiled at the angel, then said to Meg, "Thank you so much." She turned to Drew. "And thank you, too."

Mike asked, "Where do you want us to put our coats?"

She pointed toward the closet. "In there, or on the chair." She turned back to the adults. "Let me introduce you all. Drew. His mom, Kathy. This is my sister, Lila." Jess said to Lila, "Drew remembers you when you were a baby."

"You're the guy Jess was speaking to the other morning."

"That's me."

Jess interrupted. "We'll be eating in about forty minutes or so. You can all have a seat in the living room and relax. I'll call you to the table when it's time."

Kathy said, "I'm more comfortable doing. Put me to work."

"Glad to have your help," Jess said with a smile.

Lila found some fresh fruit in the fridge and tossed it together. As she carried the bowl to the table, she shook her head, saying, "I hope there's enough food."

The sisters looked at each other and laughed. Jess said, "Maybe we'd better open a couple of cans of green beans?"

Jess assembled Kathy, Drew, and Lila in the kitchen. "Okay, when the roast comes out, the rolls go in. The meat 'rests' for ten minutes. By the time we're seated at the table, the rolls will be due to come out of the oven."

No one spoke. They were looking at each other.

Lila said to Drew, "She's bossy."

He nodded.

Kathy spoke up, "Nonsense. She just knows what needs doing." She went over to the sink and began washing up the used cooking implements.

"Lila? Can you pour the iced tea?" Jess smiled. "Please?"

But Lila was looking away. She asked, "Did you hear something?"

"Yeah. Someone's at the door," Drew said. "Should I get it?"

Jess nodded, her lower lip suddenly caught between her teeth.

He leaned close and whispered, "Are you okay?"

She nodded yes, but didn't speak.

He gave her a curious look but went to the door.

"Hi, sorry, is this the right house?" A man's voice. "Drew? Is that you? It can't be."

Guy hugs ensued as Jess watched. Rob had remembered.

Lila said, "Look over there."

At the front window, Elaine and the kids were waving and yelling, "Surprise! Merry Christmas!" They piled through the door, the kids excited and squealing.

It was a madhouse as hugs and kisses were exchanged. Delightfully so.

Rob came over with a special hug for Jess. He said, "We thought we'd surprise you, but I think we got surprised instead."

"You did, and yes, you did." She laughed and shook her head. "Both."

"Just so you know, I can't guarantee the kids are disease-free. Don't blame me if any of you come down sick."

Jess hugged Elaine and the kids. "I can't believe you came all this way for one day. At least you'll get to sleep a night at the beach before heading back." She signaled to Lila. "Can you introduce everyone while I grab more plates?"

Kathy said, "I'll run next door and get extra plates and utensils."

Five more plates. A total of twelve. While she waited for Kathy to return, Jess moved the place settings very close together. It was a long table, thank goodness, but even so they'd be elbow to elbow. Somebody might have to stand at the counter. There was no room left. Not even for one more.

Unless...

She looked over at the door. It was too much to hope for. Her mother was still at sea. Jess had been so unhappy about her going, she hadn't thought to ask how long the cruise would last, but Mama had made it clear she wouldn't be here for Christmas.

Jess moved aside as Kathy returned and took over counting and arranging plates. She noticed the dishes didn't match, but she was grateful to have them.

Rob said, "The kids want to run down to the ocean. Is there time?"

"Ten minutes," Jess said. "Ten minutes only. Wear your coats." She pointed to the tallest one, Drew's nephew. "Mike, when I call, y'all come right away."

"Yes, ma'am."

"Jess." Rob touched her arm. "I'm glad you were able to get a tree, but I have to ask, why is it in the middle of the room?"

She grinned at her brother and asked, "Why not?"

A waft of fresh air entered as the kids exited. It was impressive sight—six children, most of them elementary-age and kindergarteners—thundering through to the porch and racing along the crossover. Jess followed them out, but slowly. The cooler air brushed her cheeks, reinvigorated her and helped her re-center herself.

Someone was standing on the steps at the end of the crossover.

Jess walked slowly toward him. He was standing by the steps as if he'd moved when the kids had barreled past and now didn't know what to do.

He looked back and saw her.

Lila was right. Jess didn't care about Pete. But Lila was wrong, too. She wasn't jealous and she didn't want to control everyone. She wanted the best for her loved ones, even if it cost her some pride.

"Pete. Lila said you'd gone."

"I did. I just didn't go far."

"Would you like to join us for Christmas dinner?"

He looked around, then, surprised, he pointed at his chest.

She said, "I'm serious."

"You sure?"

"I am."

"I'd like that."

"Okay, then. There's only a few minutes before dinner's ready so you should get on inside."

"Thanks, Jess."

"Don't mention it. I mean, really don't."

Pete nodded with a half-smile on his lips and walked on past.

Jess turned around and there stood Drew. "Do you know about Pete?"

"Some. You two had that...conversation on the crossover."

"We did. Hard to miss a Dawson heart-to-heart, isn't it? We're so subtle."

Drew watched the kids running on the beach, then turned to her and held out his arm. "May I?"

She nodded. He put his arm around her shoulders and said, "Seems like things didn't work out as planned this Christmas."

Jess turned toward him, her hand on his chest, and looked up at his face. "Seems like."

"Hope you're not too disappointed."

"Oh, I'm pretty tough. I can bear up under it." She leaned against him and said, "By the way, the count is now up to thirteen. I need more chairs. Can you spare a few?"

"Yes ma'am."

She pushed away from him. "The roast. I have to take it out of the oven or it'll be overdone."

"Mom's watching it."

He wasn't expecting the move, so she stood on tiptoe and kissed his cheek. But then, apparently he was expecting it, because he turned his head. His lips met hers and lingered for a while.

Jess whispered, "The roast." She yelled, "Kids. Come in."

They parted at the privacy panel. Drew went to fetch extra chairs. Jess rushed inside.

Kathy saw her and waved, saying, "No worries. I got it."

Jess joined her at the counter, quickly pronounced the roast as ready, and checked on the rolls turning golden brown in the oven.

The children scrambled back inside, but the adults were just standing around, bunched in a group. Annoyed, Jess clapped her hands. "Please, everyone, come to the table. Drew's bringing more chairs."

No one moved. Jess realized Rob and the others were smiling at her.

Two women stepped out from behind him. One said, "The ship had engine trouble and came back early."

Mama and Aunt Lucy.

Jess laughed and put her hands over her heart. "We need two more plates."

Lila said, "It's already taken care of, sis."

Drew asked, "Need more chairs?"

She slid her arm around him and said, "No, we're good. Better than good."

Not enough room at the table for thirteen? Well, fifteen would fit fine. Jess called that a buffet.

The table wasn't perfectly decorated, the dishes

didn't match, and the food assortment was a bit haphazard, but they had everything that was needed—family, friends and food, and best of all, love.

THE END

BEACH TOWEL

August—the height of beach season—yet as I drove across the bridge into the town of Emerald Isle, the streets seemed unusually quiet. Perhaps in waiting mode? The roads were wet so I knew a shower had recently moved through, but blue sky peeked from between white fluffs of clouds like a promise. Beach weather could be glorious or brooding, and there was comfort in both. I arrived at the property management office at closing time. I dashed in, apologizing, to the property manager who was about to lock the door.

"I'm sorry to be so last minute," I said. "Any chance you have something, anything, available? I'll take whatever."

The two ladies behind the counter looked at each other in silent communication. The manager, an older woman with a kind face, looked like she was shaping her lips to say no.

Quickly, I added, not able to hide the humiliating desperation in my voice, "I've had a very difficult day."

The manager said, "Did you check the hotels?"

There weren't many hotels here and that wasn't what I wanted anyway. I wanted a house, a home, even if it was a rental. I'd just fled a hotel on the mainland and didn't want anything remotely similar to remind me.

"Please. A house or a duplex? Whatever you have."

"There's a hurricane on the way. You know that, right? We aren't in the direct path, not at this time, but close to it and hurricanes can be unpredictable. It could impact your visit."

I'd already been through an event so personally dreadful and devastating that I laughed out loud at the prospect of a storm. What was a little wind and rain?

"No refunds. Just want to be clear about it."

Hope bloomed. "Yes, ma'am. Whatever you have."

"Well, let's take a look..."

I left with a key. The on-call person would drop sheets and towels off at the rental this evening. After a quick trip to the grocery store, I went directly to my hiding place.

The duplex was a small, second floor unit, and oceanfront. I was lucky to get it despite the weather threat. We were already into the rental week, so I had a prorated rate and four days—four days to figure out how I was going to fix the disaster that had become my life.

I dropped my duffel bag on a chair, shoved the garment bag into the closet and opened the balcony door wide. Salt air rushed in, bringing heat and the freshness of oceanfront North Carolina with it.

The cell phone rang. Again. His ring. Andrew's.

Shivers gripped and held me and turned my stomach. When the ringing stopped, I changed the volume to mute and tossed the phone into a drawer. Eventually, the power would drain—as my own hurt and anger would diminish, given time. I was counting on it.

Before I ran away, I'd told them all—everyone who happened to be within earshot of my shriek—that I was leaving. Don't follow me. Leave me alone. And I meant it.

****

At dawn, I put on shorts, a tank top and my running shoes. I went straight out the door, over the crossover and onto the beach.

The morning mist was lifting. Sea birds skimmed the waves for breakfast. They flew west as I ran toward the sunrise. The beach was smooth where the ocean had groomed it. I ran in the firm damp sand near to where the waves had stretched their farthest before the tide receded. With each step the sand kicked up behind me occasionally pelting my calves. Soon I was speeding along in semi-rhythm to the waves, each step making a whisk-whisk sound against the sand.

Running, breathing, running—the no-room-for-thinking kind of running that shut out emotions and deep thought— the purest form of running away.

Endorphins or the wondrous sunrise, whichever, I was feeling good, and then the whisk-whisk changed. I hadn't altered stride. I glanced back over my shoulder and that one break in concentration sent me sprawling.

Elbows hit, knees hit. I plunged forward digging rough trenches for what seemed like forever and in slow motion. When I ceased moving, the waves, foaming only inches from my face, streamed back to the ocean and gave the illusion of continued movement. Disoriented, I was having trouble righting myself when masculine knees sank into the wet sand beside me.

"Are you okay? Are you hurt?"

I pushed up slowly, wiping sand from my cheeks. My tank top was soaked and my shorts were twisted.

The man, dark-haired, red-faced, asked again, "Are you hurt?"

"I'm okay." I accepted his muscled arm and stood gingerly. My legs worked. Nothing seemed broken. "I heard something behind me. You, I guess. I don't know what happened." Then it hit me. "YOU! What are you doing here?" I pushed him hard in the chest and he took a step back.

"What am I doing here? I'm helping you get on your feet." He reached down and tugged at the edge of a bowl-like depression in the sand. Pink terrycloth emerged. "Looks like the remains of a sand castle and a beach towel. I saw it just as you hit it."

"Leave me alone. I can't believe… No, just go."

Without a hint of a smile, Jay said, "As you wish." He turned away and jogged off, gradually picking up speed.

If I could have, I would've taken off like a rocket— going the other way. However, running was out of the question because my shorts had collected a bucket load of sand and my shoes felt like they were filled with sandpaper.

How had Jay found me here? And why? He might be Andrew's dearest friend, but he was a stranger to me. I'd met him once and then seen him a second time—the day it all went bad.

I kicked my shoes off and carried them into the water. I shivered while the ocean reclaimed some of its real estate. The cold waves breaking around my waist cooled the worst of my anger. Finally, I slogged out of the ocean and stared down the beach strand.

No sign of Jay. Good. Where was he staying? How had he found me?

He knew I was a runner. I preferred to run in the morning, but how would he know that unless Andrew had told him?

I knelt at the spot where I'd fallen. The waves had already erased the evidence except for the pink beach towel still stuck in the sand. I pulled it free. It was actually a nice, plush towel, but clammy and sand-heavy. I looked around. No one. Leaving it on the beach seemed untidy. Certainly, it was dangerous.

I'd left home so quickly I hadn't brought a beach towel. Now, I claimed this one, but it was lousy compensation for my berserker fall.

A swish in the ocean removed the bulk of the sand from

the towel.

Jay couldn't know where I was staying and I would keep it that way. After another long, searching look down the length of the beach, I decided it was safe to return to the duplex.

Showered and dressed, I tossed the wet clothes and the towel into the wash and went out for breakfast. Mike's Restaurant was busy, but I didn't mind waiting. The food was good and there was no better place in which to disappear into a crowd than here at this hour of the morning. Plus Mike's held good memories for me from when Grams and Grampa lived on the island.

Their house had been on the sound side. Dad sold it when they died. We lost them within two months of each other.

My grandparents had set me up for disappointment, I thought, only half-joking, as I followed the waitress to a table. They set a standard for marriage that, I could see now, might be impossible to achieve.

All around me was chatter about the weather. Would it or wouldn't it? But that was from the vacationers. I could tell by the faces of the locals that they had already figured it out and what I saw reassured me.

I sat, gave the waitress my order, took a book from my bag and settled in. No one could mistake I wanted to be alone.

"Hi, Carrie. Mind if I sit here? This place is packed."

Dark hair, slightly less red-faced, the runner—Andrew's best man, Jay—stood there with a friendly smile. He wore khaki shorts and a beachy t-shirt. With his relaxed and sunny demeanor, he looked like he belonged here. No one would have suspected him of devious intent, except I knew better.

"Why are you following me?"

"I'm not." He shrugged. He leaned into my personal

97

space and spoke in a low tone of voice as if intending to ensure privacy, but while doing so he deftly pulled out a chair and slid into it. "I admit that I did follow you to Emerald Isle, but it was just luck that I saw you this morning and that I'm at Mike's for breakfast same time as you."

"Andrew sent you. You go back and tell him he's out of my life."

"He didn't send me."

I closed my book with a slap. "Why are you even involved? We hardly know each other. You're Andrew's friend. His best man. If he didn't send you, then why are you here?"

Yesterday morning this man, Jay, had been in a tuxedo and standing at the changing room door when I stormed through to confront Andrew. The memory hurt. It was a physical pain that tore at me each time it slashed through my brain.

"Listen carefully. I don't need people, especially not supposed friends and family, and definitely not male people, cluttering up my life, bringing crap into my life."

Those last words ended on a high, shrill note and diners at nearby tables looked up and stared. I lowered my voice and pushed my chair away from the table. It squeaked along the vinyl tiles.

"I don't care whether you're here deliberately or by chance. Leave me alone."

As I moved away from the table there was a tug on my tote bag, but I didn't grasp the significance of it until the chair crashed to the floor in my wake. I didn't stop. I moved faster. The waitress gaped as I rushed past her to the exit.

"Cancel my order," I said.

Frantic thoughts tore at me. A spectacle in public. Discourteous. Unfeeling. A quitter. Chose foolishly. Not good enough to be loved. I jumped into my car and sped off. I didn't slow down until I arrived at the duplex, and even then I was driven.

I threw open the balcony doors trying to find some oxygen. I was grateful for the wind on my face, but it gave me no peace. I went to the coat closet and dragged the garment bag out. I ripped the zipper open. White satin burst through the opening and lace spilled out with it. I pulled the gown from its hanger in a flurry of seed pearls, satin and lace, and threw it across the room. The wind, blowing through the open balcony door, suddenly whipped up a vortex and the dress billowed and swooped toward it.

I dashed after the white cloud of satin and lace, snagging the hem of the skirt as my dress tried to fly over the balcony railing.

Did I still want it? NO, but my knees buckled and I collapsed onto the warm decking of the balcony floor, clutching the dress to me, rocking back and forth. The feel of the satin spilling across my arms and bare legs was too familiar, too much like the day before. Harsh, angry voices shouted from the folds, distorted and ripping my heart. "What do you mean you're not going through with the wedding?" My stepmother's voice haranguing, "Selfish... Your father spent... Your father's business associates are... The dress alone cost..." And before that, Andrew, cornered, his deep voice saying he was sorry, but, "you should've known this would happen. It wasn't really over between Deb and me and then you asked her to be a bridesmaid. You should've known something like this could happen...but it's over now. It was a mistake and..." And before that, Deb's voice after she'd helped me to dress, shaking and saying, "Carrie, can I talk to you privately? I drank too much last night. I'm sorry. I have to tell you what happened after the rehearsal dinner. You'll

99

hate me, I know you will, but I have to clear my conscience before it's too late…"

I crushed the fabric to me and felt a scream rising from the pit of my stomach, squelched only by the sound of children laughing nearby. I buried my face in white satin.

Before I'd left them all behind me—the wedding party, the guests, the presents, the true love I thought I had—I sent a broadcast text stating wedding xcled going away leave me alone. That, of course, was in addition to my parting shriek.

Back home, in haste, I threw clothing and toiletries into a duffle bag. Get in and get out before anyone could follow me here. When I tossed the duffle into the trunk, I discovered that, in my hysteria, somehow, the garment bag had ended up there. I slammed the trunk shut.

There was only one place to run. Emerald Isle. The place, idyllic in my memory, where I'd visited my dad's parents, Grams and Grampa, every summer, and winter holidays, too, until they died.

Their home had been sold and someone else put their personal touches on the house, but the ocean was unchanging. Sand might shift with wind or tide, but it didn't really change, it just rearranged itself.

And here I was, pathetic, crouched on the balcony of a rented duplex with my bridal gown pooled around my legs.

Now, what?

I stood and shook out the folds of the gown. I arranged it on the hanger and hung it in the closet, defeated.

The clothes went into the dryer and the large, heavy towel went onto the balcony to dry. I found some clothespins in a drawer and secured it to the railing.

In the afternoon, I walked along the beach. Unless Jay intended to haunt the many miles of sand, what were the odds he'd find me again? He'd gotten lucky before. Luck wasn't likely to repeat. If it did, well, I didn't regret what I'd said to him. I didn't.

A man and woman strolled hand in hand. The scene brought me to a halt. She was barefoot; he wore sandals. Their movements were so in unison, the little gestures so attuned, that it was like a relaxed, unconscious dance. Anyone could see they'd been doing the same thing for years. I started walking again and as the distance closed, I saw how thin the man was, perhaps ill. He was several years older than the woman. She was closer to my own age. There seemed to be a story there, perhaps a sad one, but there was also contentment, and I envied them.

Where was I going with my life? I couldn't see my way out of this. How would I find my way back to happiness?

The next morning I slept in and didn't go running. I hoped that when he didn't find me, Jay would give up and go home. I had planned to go swimming in the afternoon, but the waves were increasing in force and the beach patrols had picked up, so instead I walked knee-deep amid the waves. The foaming water churned against my legs and then rushed to sea, forcing the sand from under and around my feet. I lost my footing and stumbled around trying not to fall. I failed a few times, but each time made it to my feet again. The stubborn combat with nature matched my mood.

When I returned to my duplex I clipped the towel onto the railing to dry. There'd been no sign of Jay all day long. A tiny edge of melancholy touched me. I wanted to avoid him, right? So was I disappointed? What did he mean to me?

Jay represented…what? My erstwhile groom and the friends and family who'd let me down? And maybe a tiny sliver of hope they would try to make it right? There was also something about my own behavior I had to face—something that smelled suspiciously like guilty relief.

I resumed running on the third morning and didn't hear him coming. Swiftly, he passed me without stopping, as if I wasn't even there. I slowed, then picked up my pace, legs pumping. He was a strong runner. My muscles tightened, my lungs burned and I was never going to catch him, not even if I chased him the full length of Bogue Banks. With the last scrap of air in my lungs, I called, "Jay!"

He didn't hear me. He kept going and his pace didn't vary. I slowed to a stop, bent over, hands on my thighs, and walked in a circle to keep my muscles from seizing up while I recovered from that last, strenuous sprint.

He had heard me. He was returning. When Jay stopped, he started to speak. I held up my hand, "No, wait. Please." Breathe. "I'm sorry."

"Don't be. I don't blame you. I had no right to follow you here. No hard feelings."

Dark heavy clouds rode the horizon, ominous but not worrisome because the hurricane had weakened to a tropical storm and was making a slow turn northeast.

I stood upright and drew in a last deep breath as I gathered my words. I asked, "Why are you here?"

"Not to bother you or to ask you to come back. Just to make sure you're okay."

"Okay? My dear friends and family. My fiancé. Every last one of them cared more about the wedding and their own agendas than about me. Everything was for the sake of the wedding, for money and family pride."

"What about your dad?"

I moved to dryer sand and sat. "So he's the one who sent you. He could've guessed where I'd be."

"He didn't send me. He did tell me where to look." He dropped down onto the sand beside me. "When you blasted past me to get to Andrew—nice wedding dress, by the way—

and then stormed out again, I went to your dad and asked where you'd be most likely to go. He told me. The rest was dumb luck."

"That dress. Somehow it ended up in the car trunk. It's following me around like an albatross."

"Hey, it's a nice dress—all white and everything. Don't blame the dress. It's as pointless as.... It's as pointless as blaming a beach towel because you weren't watching where you were running."

"Huh, well that was your fault anyway. You snuck up behind me." I blinked quickly, several times, feeling the sting of tears in my eyes. "I'm better off leaving them all behind and starting over somewhere else. I'm better off without them."

He didn't say anything. We sat in for a while watching the waves.

Finally, I said, "Thanks for listening."

"Happy to." He smiled. "Would you like to walk to the pier for lunch later?"

"For lunch? Why? I don't remember any great cuisine there."

"We'll take a chance and scavenge whatever we find. It's not exactly a wasteland up that way."

I didn't know what to say.

"Silence is consent. I'll pick you up at noon."

"You don't know where I'm staying."

"Of course I do. You hung that pink beach towel from your balcony like a flag. How could I miss it?" He stared down at the sand, and then at her. "I'm not buying that your dad cared more about the wedding than you."

I sighed. "I didn't give him the chance to express himself one way or the other. I couldn't face him. Not after everything he'd said, warning me, telling me he didn't trust

Andrew, yet in the end, he gave me everything I wanted. The wedding of a lifetime. And for what? I don't remember why it ever seemed like a good idea." In a softer voice, I whispered, "Or when it stopped seeming good. The last bit, between him and Deb, just sealed it."

"So why would you go through with the wedding if you weren't sure?"

A handful of sand dribbled through my fingers. "It built so fast, like a freight train. Everyone was full speed ahead. When I came to my senses, the wedding arrangements had gone so far forward, I didn't know how to jump off."

****

The wind had picked up and had a chill to it. August seemed to have fled. I hadn't packed a jacket, so I grabbed the pink towel on the way out. I put it around my shoulders like a shawl and met Jay on the beach in front of my duplex at high noon. We walked the sandy mile to the pier, mostly in quiet and fighting the gusts. There were no swimmers, not today with the waves being so rough. Along the way, I saw a man and woman on a porch, holding each other, using the house as a buffer from the wind.

"I saw them walking on the beach before. That's what I want, the kind of love my grandparents shared. I want that contentment and friendship and comfort along with the passion."

Jay laughed. "Contentment? Are you kidding me? Then why did you want to marry Andrew? Didn't you know him at all?"

"How can you say that? You're his friend."

"Yes, we're friends. For years. But I wouldn't marry him. Scratch that. I mean I wouldn't let my sister marry him, or a friend either."

"Don't you feel disloyal? Being here and saying these

things?" And coming on to his ex-bride, I wanted to say, but didn't.

"Look, I've been overseas for a couple of years, so I haven't seen as much of him as I used to, but I think you did Andrew a big favor by not marrying him. You saved him, yourself and a lot of others, major heartache down the road."

He continued, "Andrew's a good guy and he was always a lot of fun to hang around with, but that's not marriage."

"Pride, time and money—down the drain. Per my stepmom. And I can't dispute it."

We were walking west and being buffeted by the wind. I kept my beach towel around me, occasionally using it to shield my face from stinging sand. From somewhere, a woman's hat sailed overhead.

"I guess we look stupid out here, don't we?" I gripped the towel more tightly.

The pier was closed due to the weather. We found a protected spot next to a building and sat for a while, watching the angry clouds scoot by and the ever-angrier waves thrash the shore.

"If you're not here for Andrew or my father, then for who?" I stared straight ahead.

"For you. For me. I'm sorry. I wish I could say my motives were pure." He touched my arm. "I saw you before we were officially introduced, remember? When I arrived at the hotel you were returning from a run. You looked so..."

"Sweaty? Disheveled?"

"Alive. Full of life. I knew you had to be connected to the wedding. I just knew it. Figured you were a bridesmaid or something. I was going to check in, find Andrew, and ask him where I could find the amazing woman I'd just seen."

I looked down to hide the fear in my eyes and the tiny smile on my lips. I said, "I think we should go back now."

"Imagine what went through my mind when he introduced us."

I shook my head. "Can't begin to."

"No? Well, I'll tell you all about it one day."

We continued walking, lunch forgotten. He didn't ask what I thought about his declaration. I was glad because I truly didn't know. We didn't walk much further before we turned and retraced our path.

In front of the house where I'd seen the couple on the porch, the young woman now knelt on the beach near the water's edge. Shock was etched in her posture and in the wet, wild hair. Her face was hidden, pressed against her knees.

The red Beach Patrol buggy was nearby and local police officers intermingled with men whose hats showed the initials, BP. A man and woman were engaged in earnest conversation with them and there were other onlookers. I watched as the man approached the kneeling woman and spoke to her. An officer did the same, but she only clutched her bent knees more tightly. When she looked up, she stared out at the vast Atlantic.

I shuddered and pulled my beach towel more closely about my shoulders. I wasn't cold from the wind. The chill was all internal.

"Someone drowned." Jay said softly behind me. He touched my arms. "Are you okay?"

I shook my head, then nodded. "I didn't think about it before, but trouble's relative, isn't it?"

"Yeah, I think so."

"We walked through here not that long ago."

"Life can change in an instant, I know that. And no one's ever prepared."

I felt useless standing there, yet unable to turn my back and resume my day as if this was nothing. My feet, heavy, dragged through the soft sand as I went to the woman. An aura of loss surrounded her and when I reached her there on the damp sand, her grief was so raw it made my heart ache. I knelt beside her and draped my towel around her shoulders.

She looked up briefly. Her deep blue eyes went from lost to something else, like awareness. She murmured, "Thanks," then put her face against her knees again.

The 'something else' in her eyes—it terrified me. I never wanted to experience anything dreadful enough to put that look in my eyes, or to be able to recognize and understand the depth of such despair.

I scanned the area around us for the thin man I'd seen her with. He wasn't there.

Of course, he wasn't.

Overwhelmed, I scrambled away and ran blindly down the beach, my eyes blind and burning. I ran from grief, from guilt, from anger, all of the demons that fed upon me like parasites. Many yards down the beach, as my sobbing eased, I heard the whish-whish of running steps in unison with mine. I stumbled, and tried to regaining my balance in knee-deep water, ocean water—waves that came and went in eternal, heartless rhythm.

He caught me and wrapped his arms around me. I put mine around his neck and cried the rest of my tears onto his t-shirt.

A few minutes later, my tears spent, I said, "Jay, I don't know if I'm ready to date someone new. I do know that I don't want to go from one kind of trouble to another. You understand that?"

He tightened his arms. "I can't promise to be trouble-free. Is it worth the risk to find out?"

****

The storm stayed offshore. As it passed our latitude, we

suffered a few gusts and spates of rain from the outer bands during the night, but they were no more than afterthoughts from a retreating, weakening tropical storm. It was no more than a brush with temperamental, moody weather and then the threat was gone.

I didn't fool myself. Coming to terms with heartbreak wouldn't be easy and the memory would take longer to fade than the storm, but a lot of it was up to me. It was in my hands because unhappiness couldn't be over until you put a period to it, and I would do nothing to encourage it to linger. On the contrary, better memories were about to be made and would help usher out the unwelcome ones.

Jay waited on the wooden crossover outside of my duplex. I'd told him I had something I needed to do before we went on our first official date.

I dug the cell phone out from the drawer. The power cord, too. In moments, I was able to use it. I skimmed the missed calls and texts looking for one that would mean something real, and found Dad's.

luv u. so sorry be carful come hom soon luv u

Dad didn't text, but he'd done it this once.

I hit his number and my call went to his voicemail. "Hi, Dad. I'm okay. Really okay. I'll be home soon."

I leaned over the balcony rail and called out, "Coming down."

This time, maybe alone, maybe with Jay, I was on my way to find happiness. It might not be perfect, but with effort and luck, it might be even better.

The End

I hope you enjoyed this short story and the novella, BEACH CHRISTMAS. If you did, you might be interested in my other, full-length novels set in Emerald Isle, NC—BEACH RENTAL and BEACH WINDS.

My sincere thanks, Grace.

ABOUT THE AUTHOR

Grace Greene writes women's fiction and contemporary romance with suspense. A Virginia native, Grace has family ties to North Carolina. She writes books set in both locations.

The Emerald Isle books, Beach Rental and Beach Winds, are set in North Carolina where "It's always a good time for a love story and a trip to the beach."

Or travel down Virginia Country Roads in Kincaid's Hope, A Stranger in Wynnedower, and Cub Creek and "Take a trip to love, mystery and suspense."

Beach Rental, her debut novel, won the Booksellers Best contest in both the Traditional and Best First Book categories. Beach Rental and Beach Winds were each awarded 4.5 stars, Top Pick by RT Book Reviews magazine.

Grace lives in central Virginia. Stay current with Grace's releases and appearances. Contact her at http://www.gracegreene.com .

You'll also find Grace here:
Twitter: @Grace_Greene
Facebook:
https://www.facebook.com/GraceGreeneBooks
Goodreads: http://www.goodreads.com/Grace_Greene
Pinterest: http://www.pinterest.com/gracegreeneauth/
Amazon's Author Central:
amazon.com/author/gracegreene

Other Books by Grace Greene

If you enjoyed CUB CREEK, you might enjoy these novels:

BEACH RENTAL (Emerald Isle #1)

RT Book Reviews – Sept. 2012 - 4.5 stars TOP PICK

> No author can even come close to capturing the awe-inspiring essence of the North Carolina coast like Greene. Her debut novel seamlessly combines hope, love and faith, like the female equivalent of Nicholas Sparks. ...you'll hear the gulls overhead and the waves crashing onto shore.

Brief Description:

On the Crystal Coast of North Carolina, in the small town of Emerald Isle...

Juli Cooke, hard-working and getting nowhere fast, marries a dying man, Ben Bradshaw, for a financial settlement, not expecting he will set her on a journey of hope and love. The journey brings her to Luke Winters, a local art dealer, but Luke resents the woman who married his sick friend and warns her not to hurt Ben—and he's watching to make sure she doesn't.

Until Ben dies and the stakes change.

Framed by the timelessness of the Atlantic Ocean and the brilliant blue of the beach sky, Juli struggles against her past, the opposition of Ben's and Luke's families, and even the living reminder of her marriage—to build a future with hope and perhaps to find the love of her life—if she can survive the danger from her past.

BEACH WINDS   *(Emerald Isle #2)*

RT Book Reviews – June. 2014 - 4.5 stars TOP PICK

Greene's follow up to Beach Rental is exquisitely written with lots of emotion. Returning to Emerald Isle is like a warm reunion with an old friend. Readers will be inspired by the captivating story where we get to meet new characters and reconnect with a few familiar faces. The author highlights family relationships which many may find similar to their own, and will have you dreaming of strolling along the shore to rediscover yourself.

Brief Description:

Off-season at Emerald Isle ~ In-season for secrets of the heart

Frannie Denman has been waiting for her life to begin. After several false starts, and a couple of broken hearts, she ends up back with her mother until her elderly uncle gets sick and Frannie goes to Emerald Isle to help manage his affairs.

Frannie isn't a 'beach person,' but decides her uncle's home, *Captain's Walk,* in winter is a great place to hide from her troubles. But Frannie doesn't realize that winter is short in Emerald Isle and the beauty of the ocean and seashore can help heal anyone's heart, especially when her uncle's handyman is the handsome Brian Donovan.

Brian has troubles of his own. He sees himself and Frannie as two damaged people who aren't likely to equal a happy 'whole' but he's intrigued by this woman of contradictions.

Frannie wants to move forward with her life. To do that she needs questions answered. With the right information there's a good chance she'll be able to affect not only a change in her life, but also a change of heart.

KINCAID'S HOPE   *(Virginia Country Roads)*

A quiet, backwater town is the setting for intrigue, deception and betrayal in this exceptional sophomore offering. Greene's ability to pull the reader into the story and emotionally invest them in the characters makes this book a great read.

This is a unique modern-day romantic suspense novel, with eerie gothic tones—a well-played combination, expertly woven into the storyline.

Brief Description:

Beth Kincaid left her hot temper and unhappy childhood behind and created a life in the city free from untidy emotionalism, but even a tidy life has danger, especially when it falls apart.

In the midst of her personal disasters, Beth is called back to her hometown of Preston, a small town in southwestern Virginia, to settle her guardian's estate. There, she runs smack into the mess she'd left behind a decade earlier: her alcoholic father, the long-ago sweetheart, Michael, and the poor opinion of almost everyone in town.

As she sorts through her guardian's possessions, Beth discovers that the woman who saved her and raised her had secrets, and the truths revealed begin to chip away at her self-imposed control.

Michael is warmly attentive and Stephen, her ex-fiancé, follows her to Preston to win her back, but it is the man she doesn't know who could forever end Beth's chance to build a better, truer life.

A STRANGER IN WYNNEDOWER

(Virginia Country Roads)

<u>Bookworm Book Reviews</u> – January 2013 - 5 STARS

I loved this book! It is Beauty and the Beast meets mystery novel! The story slowly drew me in and then there were so many questions that needed answering, mysteries that needed solving! …Sit down and relax, because once you start reading this book, you won't be going anywhere for a while! Five stars for a captivating read!

<u>Brief Description:</u>

Love and suspense with a dash of Southern Gothic...

Rachel Sevier, a thirty-two year old inventory specialist, travels to Wynnedower Mansion in Virginia to find her brother who has stopped returning her calls. Instead, she finds Jack Wynne, the mansion's bad-tempered owner. He isn't happy to meet her. When her brother took off without notice, he left Jack in a lurch.

Jack has his own plans. He's tired of being responsible for everyone and everything. He wants to shake those obligations, including the old mansion. The last thing he needs is another complication, but he allows Rachel to stay while she waits for her brother to return.

At Wynnedower, Rachel becomes curious about the house and its owner. If rumors are true, the means to save Wynnedower Mansion from demolition are hidden within its walls, but the other inhabitants of Wynnedower have agendas, too. Not only may Wynnedower's treasure be stolen, but also the life of its arrogant master.

CUB CREEK

(Virginia Country Roads)

<u>Brief Description</u>:

In the heart of Virginia, where the forests hide secrets and the creeks run strong and deep ~

Libbie Havens doesn't need anyone. When she chances upon the secluded house on Cub Creek she buys it. She'll prove to her cousin Liz, and other doubters, that she can rise above her past and live happily and successfully on her own terms.

Libbie has emotional problems born of a troubled childhood. Raised by a grandmother she could never please, Libbie is more comfortable *not* being comfortable with people. She knows she's different from most. She has special gifts, or curses, but are they real? Or are they products of her history and dysfunction?

At Cub Creek Libbie makes friends and attracts the romantic interest of two local men, Dan Wheeler and Jim Mitchell. Relationships with her cousin and other family members improve dramatically and Libbie experiences true happiness—until tragedy occurs.

Having lost the good things gained at Cub Creek, Libbie must find a way to overcome her troubles, to finally rise above them and seize control of her life and future, or risk losing everything, including herself.

Thank you for purchasing

BEACH CHRISTMAS

&

BEACH TOWEL.

I hope you enjoyed them!

Other books by Grace Greene

Emerald Isle Novels

Love. Suspense. Inspiration.

BEACH RENTAL
(July 2011)

BEACH WINDS
(November 2013)

Virginia Country Roads Novels

Love. Mystery. Suspense.

CUB CREEK
(April 2014)

A STRANGER
IN WYNNEDOWER
(October 2012)

KINCAID'S HOPE
(January 2012)

www.GraceGreene.com

Made in the USA
Lexington, KY
29 October 2014